"Now, how can you possibly know about my love life?"

"Word gets around about you," Meg replied, teasing.

"Well, what do you know," Gabe said with a smile. "You've been discussing me with others."

"Don't flatter yourself—I may not be the one bringing up your name, you know."

He laughed. "I better back off right now. I know you well enough to know when my teasing is getting to you."

"You don't know as much about me as you think you do. The last time you teased me I was fourteen years old."

He tilted her chin up. "We're in a spotlight from the security light. Just in case anyone is observing us, let's make this look like the real thing."

"No one in this neighborhood is paying attention to us."

Gabe slipped his arm around her waist. "You know, Meg, we've never kissed."

He leaned closer and her heart beat faster.

When his mouth brushed hers, heat swept through her. His arms tightened around her, drawing her against his hard length as his mouth covered hers.

Oh. She was in trouble.

The Rancher's Cinderella Bride

SARA ORWIG

First published in Great Britain 2017
By Mills & Boon, an imprint of HarperCollins*Publishers*
1 London Bridge Street, London, SE1 9GF

Large Print edition 2017

© 2017 Sara Orwig

ISBN: 978-0-263-07210-5

Our policy is to use papers that are natural, renewable and recyclable products and made from wood grown in sustainable forests. The logging and manufacturing processes conform to the legal environmental regulations of the country of origin.

Printed and bound in Great Britain
by CPI Antony Rowe, Chippenham, Wiltshire

Sara Orwig, from Oklahoma, loves family, friends, dogs, books, long walks, sunny beaches and palm trees. She is married to and in love with the guy she met in college. They have three children and six grandchildren. Sara's 100th published novel was a July 2016 release. With a master's degree in English, Sara has written historical romance, mainstream fiction and contemporary romance. Sara welcomes readers on Facebook or at saraorwig.com.

To my editor, Stacy Boyd, with many thanks for your friendship and editing.

One

Gabe Callahan sat on the porch of his ranch house with his booted feet propped on a rail as he watched a red pickup race up the road and onto the circular drive in front of the house. Aldridge Landscape Design was in red letters on the side, against a white circle background. Having known the driver as far back in his life as he could remember, he couldn't imagine what could have made her so desperate to call him, let alone to drive the two hours southwest from Dallas to his ranch. Unless she had been in Downly, the nearest town and only thirty minutes away from him. For Meg the drive would be longer.

As the truck screeched to a stop, he winced and stood, walking to the top of the steps. He waited there till Megan Louise Aldridge popped out of the pickup and charged toward the porch.

"Good morning, Meg," he said, addressing her the way he had since she had been in preschool and he had been in the first grade. He nodded toward the pickup. "When are you going to learn to drive?"

She didn't laugh or even smile at his usual teasing, so whatever the problem was, it was big.

"Let's go inside," he said quietly, realizing something was really wrong. That alone was startling because Meg was usually cheerful. At least the Meg he remembered. He hadn't seen much of her the past few years.

"Let's sit in the library," he directed as he motioned her into the house.

As she walked beside him, he caught a whiff of the familiar lilac perfume she had worn since middle school. He gave her a sidelong glance. She hadn't changed much. Though she was taller now, her long pale brown hair was still held back from her forehead by a blue headband—the same style hairdo she'd worn since preschool. Her hair had always been either caught by a headband or braided in pigtails. And once again, she wore no makeup. Frank, honest, sweet—that was exactly how he'd describe the Meg he remembered. And exactly how she looked right now.

Though these days they kept in touch mainly through social media and through the grapevine, back in the day Meg had been a great friend— and in the earliest years, his best friend. As kids, she had been there for him during the bad times and he had been there for her. All that despite a family feud that had put a wedge between the Callahans and the Aldridges.

Sometime after his high school graduation, they'd begun to drift apart, seeing each other less, and to his relief, as far as he knew, neither one of them had had as many problems as they'd had growing up. At least not until now. Something was definitely wrong in her life to send her to his ranch looking as worried as she did.

He closed the double library doors, glancing

around a room that had three walls covered with shelves of books that he loved. From the day he moved in, this room had been his sanctuary. Crossing the room, he placed his hands on her slender shoulders. "It's been a long time since we've really talked, Meg. It's good to see you again."

"It's good to see you, too," she said, giving him a tight smile.

"I appreciated you coming to the memorial service for my brother and sister-in-law."

"I was sorry about Nathan and Lydia."

"Thanks. We've both lost brothers," he stated. "That isn't why you're here. I get the feeling something's wrong." He searched her eyes. "What is it? Do you need something from me?"

She looked directly into his eyes, and her expression was firm yet unreadable. Then she nodded. "Yes, Gabe, I need something. I need us to get engaged."

The laugh burst out of him like a popped balloon. "Nice one." He wasn't used to Meg being the jokester in the relationship, but he enjoyed a good laugh as much as anyone.

But Meg didn't laugh, or even smile. She merely stared at him and then said bluntly, "I want to get engaged to you for about a month. I want you to propose marriage."

So she wasn't kidding?

Not knowing what to think, he wiped away his grin and looked down at the floor while he pulled himself together. Then, frowning, he met her gaze once again. He could only manage one word. "Why?"

"To get my family off my back."

The explanation may have made perfect sense to her, but he felt as if he'd come in on the second act. He had no idea what she was talking about.

Before he could ask her to explain, she went on.

"Of course, it wouldn't be for real or for long. Just long enough to get my family to back off, settle down and let me live my life." Now her eyes went wide and he saw the emotion in them once again. She was deeply troubled. "They want me to marry and I don't want to get married. But they don't seem to care. Mom and Dad are pushing me even when they know I don't want this."

"But everyone in these parts knows we've never been in love or even dated. Why me?"

"Because you're my friend. I know we're not as close as we were, but in a lot of ways, Gabe, you're still my best friend. Who else would I turn to?"

"Meg, you're my best female friend—" He paused and studied her. "In fact, you may be my best friend except for my brothers, and I've told you secrets I haven't told them." What was he saying? Instead of strolling down memory lane with her, he needed to talk some sense into her. He took her by the hands and led her over to two chairs. "Let's sit and talk."

Clamping her lips together, she sat. Leaning back in his chair with one foot on his knee, he gazed at her. She looked about the same as she had the last time he had seen her, over a year ago. She had on a baggy gray sweatshirt, worn, faded jeans and scuffed, dusty boots. From what he'd heard through the grapevine, her landscape design business in Dallas was growing and successful.

It felt good to see her again, to talk to her again.

They'd always discussed their problems, but he had to admit, this one was a doozy. "Talk to me, Meg. What's the deal? You have a nice family."

"Not about this," she said, frowning, worry filling her big, thickly lashed dark brown eyes. Really pretty eyes. That thought surprised him because he had never been physically attracted to Meg. She wasn't his type of woman.

"I need your help," she said, leaning forward and taking his hands in her dainty ones that were as cold as ice.

"You're freezing," he said, covering her hands with his. "Calm down. I'll help you. Any way I can."

"I hope you mean that," she said in a low, intense voice. "Because I really need you to ask me to marry you."

He pulled his hands back, but she grasped them tighter. "It's temporary, very temporary," she said quickly. "I think one month should do it. And it wouldn't be a real engagement, of course." She leaned closer and her voice took on a more earnest tone. "I need your help, Gabe. Please," she begged, as if he had threatened to toss her out of his house.

He did what he did best. He tried to lighten the mood. "Hey, remember, you're talking to me—best friends since forever."

"I'm serious, Gabe, and I'm desperate."

"I believe you," he said, getting more worried.

She took a deep breath and looked as if she faced a firing squad.

"All of them—my parents and both sets of grandparents—want an heir. And they all want a grandchild."

He shrugged. "Tell them that will happen in due time."

"Time is part of the problem. They're all getting older. You know Todd, my oldest brother, is career military and he's in Afghanistan now and isn't getting married anytime soon. Caleb, my married brother, has a good part in a Broadway play alongside his wife, Nora. They don't want children to interfere with their careers," she said, rattling off her reasons and sounding more panicky with each one. "And Hank is gone," she said, a wistful note of sadness in her voice that made him want to offer sympathy again over her brother who was killed in a crash when he was flying his small plane. "My family is desperate for a baby and I'm the prime candidate."

He managed to extricate his hands and sat back. "I get that, but—"

"There's more. Someone wants to marry me and my family knows it," she said, looking distraught and sounding as if she were caught in a huge calamity.

"Who wants to marry you?"

"Justin Whelton—fourth generation of successful Dallas lawyers."

"I know Justin," Gabe said, frowning and thinking he could see why she had no interest in marrying him. Gabe had known Justin as long as Meg had known him. Their parents moved in the same social circles and now that he and Justin and Meg were grown, they crossed paths at social events. Gabe didn't like Justin and suspected he had done some underhanded things to win cases.

"Justin and I dated in high school. It meant nothing to each of us except convenience. It's the same now, but the minute we went out a few times this past year both sets of parents came up with the idea that we should marry. Justin's folks want him to marry because he has big political ambitions and they think being married would give him stability and better voter approval. And I'm the perfect candidate to be his wife as far as his parents and mine are concerned. I've told mine I don't love him but they think we would fall in love because we're apparently so compatible and we've known each other all our lives. My mistake was ever going out with him, just because he was a friend. There never has been any romance between the two of us, no more than there was any between you and me. We're friends. Period. I don't like to kiss him and we rarely have. How do you marry someone you don't like to kiss?"

He couldn't help it. Despite her seriousness, he chuckled.

"Gabe, don't you dare laugh at me. It isn't funny."

"I'm not laughing," he said, trying not to, "but I'm surprised Justin wants this if you won't kiss him. If you and I get pretend engaged, will you kiss me?"

"I'm serious here," she said, anger flaring in her big eyes.

He had to bite back another laugh and realized he shouldn't tease her now. She was too upset to see humor in it.

"Yes, I'll kiss you," she said through gritted teeth and her cheeks turned red.

He couldn't hold the grin that came that time.

"Gabe, so help me—"

Impulsively, he hugged her. "I'm teasing, Meg, and you know it. You just get so riled up that I can't resist." He released her, but not before he noticed she was soft to hug and far different from when she was a skinny middle school kid.

"His dad and grandfathers have offered him so many financial incentives—you can't imagine."

"That's no incentive if the lady doesn't like you. I'd think your family would listen if you firmly tell them you don't want to marry him."

"They're *not* listening, Gabe. That's the problem. They're all pushing, including Justin, who thinks this would help his career. He's laying the groundwork to run for the Texas legislature, but he wants to be in Washington and he thinks I would make—to quote him—'the right kind of wife.' What a reason to marry!" She grabbed Gabe's hands again. "You can't imagine the pressure my family is putting on me. Please, just think about a pretend engagement," she begged.

He kept telling himself this was ridiculous, she was exaggerating and he wanted no part of it. But as she held his hands in hers, he looked down into imploring brown eyes and felt himself sinking into quicksand.

"I'm friends with Justin's secretary, Gretchen," she went on. "She told me Justin is planning to propose at the big anniversary dance this month at the country club. If I turn him down in front of all those people and our families, it'll be dreadful."

Gabe pulled back and stood up. "Dammit, Meg. Justin isn't planning that because he loves you and wants a fun memory for you. He's doing it to get attention for himself."

"I know that." Her eyes went watery and he was afraid she'd start to cry. "You're not going to have to go through with marrying me. Just a pretend engagement for a month and then you can tell all your lady friends that it was a sham. I'll tell them if you want."

Shaking his head, he gave her a brief crooked smile. "Geez, Meg, I don't have a harem. You don't have to reassure anyone that I'm available." He ran a hand through his hair. "You've never been dishonest or hidden things from your folks in all your life. How are you going to look them in the eye and tell them we're engaged?"

She took a deep breath. "That's worried me the most, but they are really pushing me to marry a man I don't love, so I can do it and later I'll apologize and remind them that they forced me into this and I was really desperate."

"Ah, Meg, this isn't like you and it isn't like me. No one would believe us. Remember, we've never even had one date."

"They'd believe me. You know they would."

He stared down at her, the sinking feeling growing in the pit of his stomach. Much as he hated to admit it, she had a point. Meg was the most honest, frank person he had ever known, so a pretend engagement was so foreign to her way of living that people might never suspect it. But… "There is not another person on this earth that I know who could carry a pretend engagement off and get people to believe it, but I'm not sure you can, either."

"Gabe, it would only be a short time and—"

"I still say people won't believe us."

She stood up, dug in a hip pocket and pulled out a small velvet box. Opening it, she held it out to him. "They'll believe it when I announce it with this on my finger," she said.

He took the small box in his hand and looked down at a dazzling diamond ring. Then he looked at her. "Is this real?"

Her cheeks turned pink. "Of course not. I can't afford a diamond like that, but if it were real, you could afford it."

"Megan, your family doesn't like me or my family. Except for you and your brothers, the Aldridges haven't spoken to me for years." The silly feud had seen to that. Decades ago, both their fathers had been business partners, until his dad had bought out her dad and caused a rift that had never healed.

"Don't you see, Gabe? That's exactly why my plan is perfect. If they think I've gotten engaged to you, they'll back off pushing for marriage so fast," she said with a grim determination in her voice. "Just one month, Gabe."

He gazed into her big brown eyes and his spirits dropped another notch. "Ah, Meg, I just don't think it'll work. If it does, everyone will think I've gotten you pregnant."

"I don't care because in time, they'll know that you haven't. That's no problem."

"We've never had one date," he insisted.

"So we start dating. Gabe, I'm desperate," she cried.

Gabe patted her soft hand while he thought about what she had just told him. He had always promised her he would help her if she ever needed him, and he was letting her down now, when she needed him most.

Meg was relentless. Her barrage of persuasion persisted. "If we get engaged, everyone will talk about it and Justin and I will vanish from the center of conversations in our families.

"You ought to be at my house for dinner any night and hear them badgering me. My dad has offered to give us enough money to buy a house. My grandparents have offered the deed to one of the ranches they own. They're so earnest. One set of grandparents will fly me and my mom to New York for me to have a makeover and buy an entire new wardrobe. It's ridiculous."

She tightened her cold fingers around his hand, leaning closer, looking as if she would burst into tears. "Please. It's just pretend, so it doesn't matter how we feel about each other."

No matter how many reasons she gave him, he still thought the ploy wouldn't work. It would be disastrous and only make her family dislike him even more. And he wasn't sure it would help her at all. In fact, the only one he saw coming out of this well was old Justin, who'd save face by not getting rejected during a dumb public proposal.

No, he thought, *this was not a good plan at all*.

Reluctance filled him. He squeezed her shoulder gently, her soft hair falling on his hand. He looked deep into her eyes and prepared to decline, no matter how much it hurt him to not be there for her.

But he couldn't believe the words that came out of his mouth.

"I'll be your pretend fiancé if that's what you want."

The words had just spilled out. Who was he kidding? He could never resist helping her.

"Oh, Gabe, thank you," she cried, hugging him.

He wrapped his arms around her, still feeling as if she were the sister he never had. Except when he hugged her, it was a curvy woman's body pressed against him and he had a fleeting curiosity about what she'd look like out of that shapeless sweatshirt she wore. She was soft and smelled sweet, the same lilac scent he'd always remembered. As a little kid, she'd told him her grandmother got her lilac soap. He released her and gazed into brown eyes and a big smile.

"You're pretty, Meg. There ought to be all sorts of guys wanting to take you out."

She shook her head. "Not anyone I want to go out with and not anyone I'd trust with a pretend engagement. I'm probably too bossy because I'm used to running my own business and giving orders."

"I don't recall thinking you're too bossy."

A brief smile flickered on her lips. "That's because you're bossier."

"You never told me that. Well, maybe a time or two."

"You can be as bossy as you want. Thank you, Gabe."

"If we're going to do this, and you want to stave off a public proposal at the dance, let's get with it. Today is Thursday. I think we should have a first date this weekend if you can make it," he said.

"I sure can," she said, wiggling with eagerness that made him remember times in the past when she would get her way and be very happy. "Say when."

"Saturday night," he answered, wondering what she was pulling him into with this pretense and how much explaining he would have to do with some of his close female friends.

"Saturday it is."

"How are you going to tell Justin about going out with me Saturday night?"

"I won't have to yet because he's going out of town this weekend on business. He'll be back Wednesday and by that time, he'll know we went out. Even one date with you will make him call off a public proposal."

She turned to leave, but spun back around. "I almost forgot. Saturday night, do you want me to be at my house in Downly or my house in Dallas?"

"You have two houses?" he asked.

"It works out better with my landscape business. You probably don't even know I'm not living at home with my folks anymore, do you? My maternal grandparents do that."

"Which place is more convenient for you on Saturday?"

"Downly."

"Then I'll pick you up at your house in Downly. I need an address."

"I'll text you," she said. Then her eyes narrowed as she looked at him with an expression he couldn't read. "Do you think it's going to be weird to 'date'?"

"No. We've always had fun together and Saturday night won't be any different." He leaned into her, bumping her shoulder with his.

"I suppose you're right." She grinned at him, then came back with another suggestion. "Later, after a few dates, maybe I can stay at your ranch so it will look as if we're serious, and sometimes at your house in Dallas, so I can go to work from there. It won't be for long and I'll stay out of your way."

That might not be the best idea, but he couldn't say no at this point. And actually part of him looked forward to seeing her more because she was always good company. "That's fine if you want to," he finally said. "I have big houses with plenty of room."

Her grin turned into a full-fledged smile. "In case I forget to tell you this a thousand times over the rest of my life, thank you, Gabe. You always promised I could come to you for help and now you're going to help me," Meg gushed, her eyes getting a sparkle that made him feel a degree better.

"I don't want a loveless marriage and I don't want to marry Justin. None of them can understand it. When I marry, I want the love and closeness my grandparents and my parents have had."

He knew she did. That was the kind of woman Meg was.

"Then I hope this ploy works, Meg. For your sake."

"Oh, it will. You'll see. We'll convince my family and Justin's, and they're the ones who count. And then you can go on your way knowing you have been the knight to the rescue." She patted his hand. "My wonderful, handsome knight."

It might not be a role he was accustomed to, but he had to admit he was going to like it. But before he got knighted, they had a lot of work to do. He only hoped they'd pull off the charade as easily as Meg seemed to think they would.

While Meg had always been a good friend, there had never been anything romantic between them. Nor would there ever be. As great as she was, she wasn't his type and he wasn't hers. They were just too opposite. She was too staid and fearful of the daring things he liked to do. And then there was the feud between the older generations of their families. No, Meg wasn't the woman for him and he wasn't the man for her. But now they had to convince the world they were. He hoped this charade did not have to last long. He liked his other women friends and partying too much to be tied up in Meg's pretense.

She still held his gaze as she said, "You are an absolute angel coming to my rescue."

He laughed. "I've been called a lot of things, but 'angel' has never been one of them."

She smiled sweetly at him and patted his cheek. "You're definitely my angel." She ran her hand lightly over the stubble on his jaw. "You've stopped shaving close. It gives you a rugged, devil-may-care look even more than before," she said, tilting her head to study him. "I like it. You know, I wish Hank could know what a huge favor you're doing for me."

"If your brother knew, he would roll on the floor with laughter. But your family… They're going to hate me when they learn the truth."

"They don't like you now because you're a Callahan. This will get them to stop talking to me about Justin and start talking to me about breaking up with you. And Hank wouldn't roll on the floor and laugh at us. He'd thank you and tell me to go for it because he wouldn't approve of them trying to push me into a loveless marriage."

She turned to leave again.

"I better run, Gabe," she said. "Oh, I almost forgot. You keep this ring, and soon you can give it back to me to wear." She thrust the small box into his hand.

"Sure, Meg," he said, thinking he had to after all their years of friendship. She'd always been there for him when he was young and hurt by his dad. When his dad wasn't around for graduation or games or awards or holidays, she had supported him and cheered him up. "I owe you this because you stood by me when I was ignored by my dad. He never gave me or any of my brothers his love, his time or his attention. It was worse for our stepbrother, Blake, because our father didn't even acknowledge Blake as his son. At least I had your friendship when I was so hurt."

She smiled at him as she walked out to her pickup. "That's what friends are for, and you're the best I've ever had."

"I think you used that same line with me when you were nine years old," he remarked drily and she laughed. She had a contagious smile, and under ordinary circumstances it would have been good to see her again, he admitted.

"I probably talked you out of some of those fancy marbles you used to have. I thought they were the most beautiful marbles ever. I still have them."

"You always were easy to please so I guess I don't have to rack my brain over where to take you to eat on Saturday."

"This first time let's go somewhere we'll be seen and where people will talk about us."

He grinned. "Whatever you want to get this show on the road. I'll see you at seven Saturday night," he said, opening the door to her pickup.

With a quick pat on his hand, she climbed in and he closed the door. "You know, there is a way you can cut the dating time in half and end your folks pushing you to marry."

"What's that?"

He placed his arm on the door and leaned in closer. "Move in with me."

"That's actually a wonderful idea, Gabe."

He laughed. "I think we have different views of living together."

She wrinkled her nose at him. "I'm just thinking of staying under one roof."

He leaned down. "Shucks, Meg, I'm thinking about staying in the same bed. We didn't discuss that. We should have some fun with this deal."

"Will you cool it? We're not going to bed together," she said while her cheeks turned pink and he laughed.

"I've sure had worse ideas." He grinned and she shook her head, but she smiled at him.

"Stop teasing me. You haven't changed any. See you later."

Laughing, he watched her drive away and wondered how much Meg was going to complicate his life. She said this would only be a month and then it would be over. But the month was going to be interesting—Meg living in the same house with him. He was sure she was old-fashioned.

And he would try to curb some of his teasing, but it was hard to resist getting a rise out of her. All in all, he looked forward to spending the time with her. How much had she changed since she had grown up?

He turned the velvet box over in his hand, thinking about the dazzling ring that was as fake as their engagement would be. Would a month's pretend engagement really have any impact on his life?

Two

Meg closed the door of her small house in Downly, and glanced around at familiar surroundings without seeing any of them. She threw her arms up and spun on her toes, joy and relief overwhelming her. Gabe would help her. He was going along with the pretend engagement and she couldn't wait for their first date.

A date with Gabe. The thought stirred tingles of excitement that surprised her. She didn't want to feel any attraction to him. He was a wild man with wild ways. He loved the ladies. And he was not her type. Whatever excitement she felt over being with him would vanish, she was sure.

She poured a glass of water and stepped onto her patio while she thought about Saturday night. Saturday was a big day in the landscape business, but she could get off early. She wasn't going to say no to any date Gabe suggested as long as it was soon. She knew she should head to work now, but she wouldn't be able to focus on anything except jubilation that Gabe would bail her out of her problem.

She remembered how she had tried to cheer him up and comfort him as a kid when his dad wouldn't come home or ignored Gabe when he was home. Through the years, Gabe had repeatedly promised that he would help if she ever had any problems and he'd insisted she promise she would come to him with them. That was all childhood history, but he had come through on his long-ago promises to her today.

She went to the room she had turned into an office. Shelves lined the walls with books, pictures, trophies, awards and stacks of papers. She crossed the room to pick up a small picture and looked closely at it. It was a snapshot of her and Gabe in her backyard. He held her pigtail in front of his face like a mustache while he grinned at the camera. She smiled as she looked at it. "Thanks for being my friend always," she said to his picture.

She was going out with him Saturday night— their first date. But one where she needn't worry about what to wear. Gabe wouldn't care. Going out with him would be like an evening with one of her brothers. The thought reminded her of Hank again. Hank and Gabe had been close friends, and they were a lot alike. Hank had taken risks like Gabe did and had loved life on the wild side—flying, competing in rodeos, taking out party girls and never getting serious. Gabe was slightly older and her family felt he had been a bad influence on Hank. In the early years when her dad had worked with Gabe's dad in their own business, both families had been close and Hank thought Gabe was great. Later, her family was so bitter over the way Dirkson Callahan had cut her dad out of the business that they stopped speaking to any of the Callahans and didn't want any of their children to speak to them, either. While the grandparents felt the same as her parents, the feud had never carried over to her generation, and as much as possible, her generation had stayed friends with one another.

Her family wasn't going to want her to marry Gabe, and with a ring on her finger from him, she expected them to stop pushing her to marry.

She hugged the picture. "Thank you, thank you," she whispered, remembering when he had hugged her today. His broad shoulders and strong arms were a physical reassurance that made her feel safe, as if her problems were solved. She looked more intently at the picture. When had that skinny kid grown into a tall, strong man whose hug could make her feel that she was safe and all would be right with her world? He had grown up to be a good-looking guy, which she had never thought about before in her life.

"You're definitely my best friend," she whispered to his picture.

Still smiling, she placed the picture back on the shelf and went to her desk to check emails on her laptop.

Like her brother Hank who had been in commercial real estate, Gabe had gone into business with his older brother Cade in commercial real estate with a large office building in Dallas. She knew through the years they had oil and gas investments and business ties with Gabe's stepbrother, Blake, who was a hotel mogul. She didn't know whether Gabe spent more time in Dallas now or more time on his ranch. He could afford to do whatever he wanted.

Briefly, she concentrated on her emails, answering quickly and then gathering things to take to Dallas to her office, which was almost a two-hour drive away, depending on traffic. Before she left the room she blew a kiss toward Gabe's picture. "My handsome knight to my rescue," she whispered.

Relieved, happier than she had been in a couple of months, Meg gathered her things and left for her office, able to concentrate fully on business and work that she had planned for the day.

Saturday came swiftly and at the end of the day, she rushed home to get ready to go out with Gabe. She showered and dressed, selecting clothes that might get her noticed—not by Gabe but by other diners. She chose a pair of her fancy skintight jeans, her best black boots and a bright red sleeveless vee-neck shirt, and a matching red headband.

Gabe suggested they go to the best barbecue place near Downly, where they could have ribs along with some boot-scootin' fun. Because many people from Dallas were there on the weekend, word would spread back to Big D real easily. Not only would that put the kibosh on Justin's proposal, but she would have fun with Gabe in the meantime.

Promptly at seven she heard a car door slam and seconds later her doorbell rang. She hurried to open the door to Gabe, who wore a black hat, black shirt, jeans and black boots. He had never looked as appealing as he did at that moment because he was going to deliver her from a worrisome dilemma.

"Are you ready for a new adventure?" he asked, grinning at her.

"You can't imagine how ready, you handsome cowboy. I want you to sweep me off my feet."

"That sounds like my kind of task," he replied

as his gaze swept over her from head to toe. He whistled. "Wow, you grew up in the most delightful way. You look pretty."

"Thank you. I hope I'm pretty enough for people to post our picture on all sorts of social media." She reached for her keys. "I'll show you my house sometime, but right now, I can't wait to get out there and let every Texan possible see us together."

"Slow down, Meg," he said, laughing. "I promise, you'll be noticed."

Grabbing her broad-brimmed black hat, she locked up and left, walking beside him toward his shiny black pickup. "You know, I never noticed what a good-looking guy you are."

His smile widened. "You've gotten what you want, Meg, so you can cut the flattery. Or are you buttering me up for more? I'll tell you now—I agreed to a pretend engagement but I draw the line at a pretend marriage. I'm not the marrying kind, real or even pretend."

"I wouldn't think of asking you to do one more thing," she answered with exaggerated politeness.

"I seem to remember a few instances when you

turned on the sweetness and charm with a definite goal in mind."

"You exaggerate, but that's okay. With time
your memory has embellished circumstances. I
can't tell you how happy I've been the last couple of days, and how relieved. I feel as if I've es-
caped prison."

"Yeah, I've had a few relationships that I ended
and then felt the same way," he said with a smile.

She wrinkled her nose at him and shook her
head. "Well, this is a once-in-a-lifetime dilemma
for me. I will never again get myself in this kind
of situation with a guy."

"Watch what you predict. Life has a way of
sending us all kinds of surprises. Did you ever
think we'd be going out on a date?"

Shaking her head, she laughed. "I'm sure on
this one," she said as he opened the pickup door
and she slid into the seat to watch him circle
the pickup. He was good-looking, something she
hadn't given much thought to in past years. A
Dallas magazine had listed Gabe as one of the
top twenty most eligible bachelors in the area.

But Gabe's looks and sex appeal wouldn't interfere with her plans.

Tonight she just wanted to have fun, to celebrate her freedom that was coming, freedom to live her life her way without a constant war with her parents and grandparents.

Gabe drove to a log building with a long front porch. Rocking chairs and pots of blooming flowers created a relaxed, inviting ambience. Inside, lights were low, and ceiling fans turned slowly above dancers circling the floor as a fiddler and a drummer played. Gabe got a table at the edge of the dance floor where couples were already into a lively two-step.

"This is perfect. Everyone will see us at this table."

"Unless someone is blind drunk, you're probably right," Gabe remarked drily. "Now order up. And relax, Meg. You'll get what you want. You look ready to jump out of your skin."

She laughed. "I'm so excited and happy. Let's dance and then more people will see us."

Laughing, he shook his head as he stood and took her hand. In seconds, he held her hands while she danced at his side in another fast two-step. He turned her around and when he caught her to stop her from turning again, he pulled her slightly closer. Flashing another smile, she looked up at him. "You adorable man. You're the best friend possible," she said, hoping she looked like a woman falling in love.

"Don't overdo it," he said, laughing at her.

"There's no way to overdo what I feel, and since I want people to think I'm falling in love with you, I have to look as if I'm having the time of my life. Which I kind of am."

"You're shameless, Meg. I keep telling myself not to be flattered that you asked me to be your pretend fiancé, because any guy would have fit the bill. Except you knew that because of our friendship, I'd do this without any demands on you."

"Not so. I wouldn't trust any other guy. Besides, with another guy no one would believe me. But you fit all the qualifications. I've known you forever. You're handsome, sexy, fun, popular, wealthy—"

"Stop with all the flattery. You've already got

what you want. If I were all that you said, the ladies would be lined up at our table waiting to dance with me."

"I'm surprised they aren't, but they're watching you, which means they're watching us, which is good. Hey, you're a good dancer, too."

"Don't sound so surprised. What do you think I've been doing on Saturday nights?"

"Well, you just seem so into planes, motorcycles and bull riding that I didn't expect you to be so light on your feet."

"Maybe you're in for all kinds of surprises from me," he said with an exaggerated leer that made her laugh.

"Bring 'em on, cowboy. I'm ready for some excitement in my life."

"I told you before—and you know the old saying—watch what you wish for. That's a challenge you just gave me, Meg," he teased.

"I'm ready for you." She twirled and came back beside him. "It's fun to be with you again." When he was about to protest, she said, "I mean it. You have to admit, it's different from when we were little kids."

"Is it ever, darlin'. And vastly better," he said, his gaze drifting over her again, making her laugh and feel a surprising tingle.

The dance ended and he held her hand as they returned to their table. She stopped to say hello to some people on the way. As soon as they had ordered, she stood. "I'll be back in a minute. I'm going to the ladies' room."

"Yeah, I know. You're going so more people will see you."

She smiled and left, knowing that Gabe would be good-natured about this fake engagement. Excitement bubbled in her and she wondered how much of it was knowing her problem would soon be a thing of the past—and how much was just pure excitement from being with Gabe.

When she returned to their table, they ordered and shortly had platters with piles of ribs covered in red barbecue sauce, a mound of curly fries and thick, buttered Texas toast. While they ate, she tried to catch up on his current life.

As they laughed over a recent incident, Gabe took a sip of his beer and when he set it down, he smiled. "You're right—it's good to be together again," Gabe said.

"I'm surprised there's no woman in your life right now, but I'm glad there's not, otherwise you couldn't have gone out with me. Why don't you hold my hand," she suggested. "That would look good."

His grin widened. "This is the first time my date has told me how to come on to her."

"Well, I just want you to look as if you're falling in love and really want me. So far, with all the fun we're having, we look just like what we are—two old buds out together."

"Oh, darlin'," he drawled. "I think I can get beyond just buddies without you having to coach me," he said in a husky, breathy statement that was barely above a whisper. He stood, drawing her to her feet while he watched her intently. He slipped his arm around her waist, pulled her tightly against his side as they walked to the dance floor.

"Oh, my," she said, gazing up at him. "That's definitely on target."

"Just wait, darlin'." He leaned down to whisper into her ear, his warm breath stirring tingles that surprised her.

On the dance floor she turned to face him, winding her arms around his neck and gazing into his eyes as they moved in unison. Her satisfaction climbed over how well they fit together.

"Gabe, this is positively a dream come true," she said, dancing closer so he could hear her over the music. "Tanya is here, Justin's ex-girlfriend, and she's seen me. She can't stop glancing at me. When this dance ends, try to be near her and we'll go talk to her. I'll introduce you."

"Dare I hope she's the one in the skintight jeans and low-cut blue blouse that reveals a lot of her ink? No wonder his parents have focused on you. They're not the type for tats and blouses with vee necklines to the waist. As adorable as you are, I'm surprised Justin gave in so easily."

"I think I should feel insulted, but I don't. Justin's dad gave him incentives to give in. If he marries me, he gets a partnership in the firm after the first year of our marriage. If I'm pregnant, he gets an even bigger deal," she said, shivering.

"No wonder you want out of that. Damn. My dad gets an F in fatherhood, but he hasn't pulled anything like picking a wife for any of us."

"Until this, my parents have been wonderful. So have my grandparents, and I love them all dearly."

"We'll head Tanya's way. I won't protest meeting her," he said, dancing Meg her way.

The music stopped and she turned, smiling at Tanya and pulling lightly on Gabe's hand. Tanya's straight, waist-length blond hair fell loosely around her face. She wore a tight blue silk top with bling along the neckline that dipped in a deep vee, revealing half of a butterfly tattoo on the curve of her full breast. Curiosity filled her eyes as she watched Meg and Gabe approach. She glanced back and forth at each of them until Meg greeted her.

"Tanya, meet Gabe Callahan. Gabe, meet Tanya Waters."

Smiling, Tanya touched the arm of the man beside her. "Hi. This is Bobby Jack Lawrence."

As the men greeted each other, Gabe held Meg's hand lightly. They talked a moment until the music commenced again and then Gabe pulled her to his side for a two-step.

"That was absolutely perfect," Meg said. "I'm so glad we came here. I see Cassie Perkins from Justin's office. I think she's interested in Justin, so I'm sure she'll get the word out around his office."

Gabe looked down at her. "I didn't know you could be so plotting and devious."

"Only because I'm desperate," Meg said. Then she became quiet, enjoying dancing with him and thinking the evening had been a huge success.

"How in the world did you get involved with Justin in the first place?"

"Friendship. The way I am with you. We go to the same places and see each other. We like the same things—symphony, opera, contemporary art. His folks were giving him a terrible time about seeing Tanya and we talked about that. I just didn't realize what it would lead to and suddenly he was talking a marriage of convenience."

"Lesson learned there, I suppose."

"There's no danger of our families trying to push you and me into a marriage of convenience.

Actually, this ought to set family tongues wagging about us going out together and get Justin out of the conversation."

"This fake engagement sure as hell isn't going to endear me to any of your family."

"I'm sorry about that, but they don't like any Callahans anyway, so it isn't like you're losing their friendship."

"Somehow, your logic doesn't cheer me," he said and she smiled.

It was after midnight when a number ended and Gabe spun her around, catching her and pulling her up against him. She looked up into his eyes and her laughter faded, her grin giving way to a sultry smile.

He gazed back and took her hand. "That look should convince the most doubting spectator. If I didn't know better, I'd be on fire now," he remarked.

"Well, I'm thankful you didn't laugh because that definitely kills the effect."

"What I felt wasn't laughter," he said. The smoldering look he gave her made her tingle, which surprised her. How shocking that she found him so appealing.

"I think we can leave now," he said, wrapping his arm around her waist and pulling her close against his side.

She slipped her arm around his waist, looking up at him and smiling, as if they were about to go home and make love. She hoped that's what others thought.

"That was fun, Gabe. You're perfect for this. You would convince anybody that we're a couple."

"Anybody who doesn't really know you," he remarked drily. "Otherwise, I think there will be suspicion."

"No, there won't," she assured him, supremely happy with the way the evening had gone and looking up at him as if she thought he was the most adorable man on earth. At the moment that wasn't even pretend.

Gabe drove to her small home in Downly in an older part of town with tall shade trees. Her bright front light illuminated the porch, the surrounding flower beds, the steps, the walk and half of her front yard.

"That's some porch light you have. Your house hasn't been broken into, has it?"

"Heavens, no. I just like a light when I come home. It's cheerful."

He shook his head. "It's like the one at the Hansons' lumber yard at night. Well, I'd say tonight was a success."

"Definitely. Next I think we should hit the country clubs in Downly and in Dallas. I'll get dressed up so I look more like the ladies you normally take out."

He laughed. "I don't think old Justin stands a chance." After parking his pickup, Gabe stepped out to open her door.

She waited, hoping someone she knew would drive by and see them. Getting out of the pickup, she looked around. "I don't see anyone. My neighbors aren't the curious type and no one's ever on this street. Nonetheless, just in case someone is watching, I'll hang on to you, and you can put your arm around me," she said as he slipped his arm around her waist.

"This is a unique experience," he said with laughter in his voice. "Even my first date didn't tell me what to do and that was fifth grade."

Meg shook his arm playfully. "I'm not telling you what to do—at least not the entire evening," she added as they climbed the porch steps and turned to face each other. "Thank you, thank you. I am indebted to you and tonight was a roaring success," she said, smiling up at him as his hands rested on her waist.

"Meg, this night is not over yet," he drawled in a deep voice. He glanced around. "I feel like I'm onstage right now, under a spotlight." He looked up at her porch light. "I take it Justin doesn't mind the light."

"There is absolutely no reason for him to. Besides, we haven't gone out together in Downly."

"Are you going to let me kiss you?" Gabe asked, his blue eyes twinkling. "I don't think I've asked that question since my first date, either."

Knowing he was enjoying himself by teasing her, she smiled. "Yes, I will, but I'm not going to bed with you."

"Now you've flung another challenge at me that

I'm going to have to deal with," he said, flirting with her.

Still smiling at him, she shook her head. "That was no challenge. It's an established, guaranteed fact."

"Oh, Meg, sweetie," he drawled, taking her hand and stroking it lightly while his eyes still sparkled, "you've done it now. I can't wait for our next date. My reputation with the ladies may be on the line here."

"Don't be ridiculous. If you slept with me, no one would ever know it except the two of us. I know you don't talk about your affairs of the heart," she said, trying to keep from laughing and also aware that his light caresses were stirring surprising sizzles. How could Gabe cause any sizzles? He had always been like a brother. She gazed more intently at him, thinking that brother image was being melted away by every stroke on her hand.

"Now, how can you possibly know about my love life?" he asked.

"Word gets around about you."

"Well, what do you know—you've been discussing me with others."

"Don't flatter yourself. I may not be the one bringing up your name, you know."

He laughed. "I better back off right now. I know you well enough to know when my teasing is getting to you."

"You don't know zip about the grown-up me. We haven't spent much time together since I was a teenager."

He didn't respond to that remark. Instead, he was focused on something else. "Let's go back to my question."

She knew the one he meant. *Are you going to let me kiss you.*

He tilted her chin up. "We're in a spotlight. Just in case anyone observes, let's make this look like the real thing."

"No one in this neighborhood will observe us," she said, amused, curious about kissing him.

Gabe slipped his arm around her waist. "You know, Meg, we've never kissed," he said, looking into her eyes.

She gazed back into vivid blue eyes that seemed

to turn her insides to jelly. Gabe really was a good-looking man. When his gaze shifted to her mouth, to her amazement flutters tickled her insides.

He leaned closer, slowly, and her heart beat faster. When his mouth brushed hers, heat engulfed her. She closed her eyes, winding her arm around his neck. His arms tightened around her, drawing her against his hard length as his mouth covered hers and his tongue stroked hers.

She felt in free fall, her insides clenching while her heart pounded. She forgot everything except his kiss, his arms holding her tightly and their bodies pressed together. Tingles raced through her and she moaned softly with pleasure, sinking into a kiss that set her ablaze. Sliding her hand across his shoulders, she trailed her fingers over his nape and into his thick hair.

She had no idea how long they kissed. She only knew she didn't want to stop. When he finally raised his head, he gazed silently into her eyes and she felt as if she were seeing him for the first time in her life.

"Wow," she whispered. "Now I know why the

ladies like you," she said, trying to keep the moment light though she was stunned how his kiss had ignited such desire in her. She stepped back and from the look of him, he was as surprised as she felt.

"Thank you, Gabe, for tonight," she said, or hoped she said. Her thoughts were still on his kiss and she fought an urge to walk back into his arms and kiss him again. "I had a wonderful time and we were seen by so many people." She felt as if she was babbling, but she couldn't think straight. Gabe's kiss had scrambled her thoughts and she was trying to return to the world as it had been before he held her tightly and kissed her.

"I think this fake engagement is going to be easier to do than I first thought it would," he remarked drily, still looking intently at her. "You and I wasted our time playing with marbles."

"Not really. Our friendship was important. Tonight was perfect and a million thank-yous for agreeing to the engagement."

"I'm beginning to look forward to it. I'll call you. I'll try to plan something where you'll be seen by another segment of people you might know."

"That would be excellent. I'll get a fancy dress for the occasion. I'll even wear makeup."

He grinned and touched the tip of her nose. "I like you the way you are. You know, now I'm glad you called me for help, and believe me, I'm willing to help you."

"Thanks. Calm down a little, Gabe."

"After our kiss? I don't think so, darlin'. Want to try again and see if we get the same result?"

She leaned closer and squinted her eyes to look at him as she poked his chest with her forefinger. "We're not going to fall in love."

The twinkle was back in his blue eyes. "You don't think?"

"I know. You can't get serious and I definitely will not get serious with you."

"That doesn't mean we have to avoid kissing, does it?"

"I know you're laughing at me again. No, it doesn't mean we won't kiss. Maybe all the ladies you kiss fall in love with you, but I won't, so yes, we can kiss."

"I'm so glad to get your permission," he said, his voice filled with so much laughter she had to smile. "You've given me another challenge, Meg."

"Oh, no. Once again, that's a fact. I'm not going to fall in love with you and you won't with me. We're definite opposites. Good night, Gabe. Thank you, and it was fun."

"Oh, darlin', was it ever fun," he said, suddenly sounding sincere.

She turned to unlock her door. "I don't think I'll invite you in tonight. We'll save that for next time, when I'll show you my house."

"Sure, Meg. I'll call you," he repeated as he headed toward the steps.

As he drove away, she closed and locked the door and leaned against it, lost in memories of his kiss. How could his kiss have been so sexy? Her lips still tingled and she wished she could have gone on kissing him. Had she gotten herself into a predicament with this fake engagement?

It had never occurred to her she would have the slightest sexual response to Gabe. She had never even thought about kissing him. She had known him all her life without that happening and she hadn't given it a thought.

Till now.

Tonight he had turned her world upside down. And she no longer saw him the way she had before. Would she ever in her life see him again without that hot, tingling response she felt?

Gabe would be aiming for seduction. As he said, he liked a challenge. He also liked the ladies and parties…and a daredevil lifestyle that took her breath away, because it was the same as her brother Hank's lifestyle had been, and that wild living had gotten him killed.

Surely she wouldn't succumb to Gabe; she wouldn't go to bed with him. She had known him all her life and would never run the risk. One hot kiss wouldn't make a difference.

Except his kiss was different from all other kisses she had ever experienced. Not that there had been lots of different guys, but she suspected if there had been, Gabe's kiss still would have melted her. "Mercy me," she groaned. The man was sinfully sexy, and she suspected she'd never view him the way she once had again.

What was she saying? She could not be attracted to Gabe. Absolutely not! Kisses were one thing. Falling into bed with him was another.

She moved through her house, switching off lights and going to her room. She just needed some sleep. But when she crawled into bed, sleep was the last thing on her mind. She lay there, gazing into the darkness, her lips still tingling and memories burning their way into her thoughts. She may not want to admit it, but she still wanted to kiss him again.

She sat up in bed. "I'm not going to fall into bed with you," she whispered in the darkness. That wild, woman-chasing cowboy would be nothing but heartbreak. It was just one month. One month wasn't a long time. Surely she could resist him for that long. It could be a lot of kisses though, because it wasn't going to be just weekend dates. She planned to stay at his house with him. She'd simply have to guard her heart and keep kisses to a minimum.

Did she have the willpower for that? She suspected it was going to be difficult to resist him. He wouldn't have trouble resisting her, so maybe there was nothing to worry about. She just had to take care, remember who he was and how he felt about a serious relationship, and that wild lifestyle he had. He raised rodeo bulls for a living—big, mean, thousand-pound animals. He liked to compete in bull riding. He flew his own plane. He had a motorcycle and a sports car. And he loved the ladies and parties. There wasn't a serious bone in his body.

She had to make each date move things along to convince her family and Justin that she and Gabe were serious. The minute Justin was out of her life, she would thank Gabe and send the sexy hunk on his way.

When had Gabe changed to a "sexy hunk" from the friendly kid she grew up knowing? She hadn't been around him in the past few years because they moved in different circles after school. She knew a lot of local ladies loved going out with him. She paid little attention when one of her friends talked about wanting to date him. Such conversations left her slightly amused at most. But his kiss wasn't amusing. It was sexy enough to wrap around her heart and carry it away.

She punched her pillow behind her, feeling suddenly uncomfortable. "You may be my knight to the rescue, Gabe Callahan, but you're going to be trouble," she said in the dark, empty room. Moonlight spilled in the window. All she could see was Gabe's blue eyes and his cocky smile. "About six feet, three inches of sexy male and you've already rocked my life. We'll kiss, but I will not go to bed with you. I mean that," she whispered, and sighed. She knew she'd better stick to that conviction if she wanted to get through this pretend engagement with her heart intact.

She sighed again, getting up and opening a bottom drawer to rummage through sweaters. She pulled out a raggedy brown bear and shook it. Gabe had given it to her on her ninth birthday. "Why didn't he stay the way he was when he gave you to me?" she asked the bear. "A nice kid I had fun with instead of this sexy man who makes me want to keep kissing him all night."

She hugged the bear that she had loved ever since receiving it, even taking it to college with her.

She went back to bed and sat cross-legged, putting the bear in front of her. "I will get through this engagement and Gabe and I will have fun like we always have. I will not go to bed with him and when the month is over—or hopefully, sooner—I will thank him, give him a big present and we'll go our separate ways. I am not going to fall in love with him like one of his women he's had an affair with." She poked the brown bear with her finger. "I promise and you're my witness."

She'd bet anything that Gabe hadn't even thought about their date or their kiss or anything else about her. He was probably wishing this month would zip on past. Either that or peacefully sleeping.

She'd asked him to take her somewhere fancy next time and told him she would look more like the women he usually dated. Right now, she was a million miles from that look, but wonders could be achieved with the right makeup, a new hairstyle and some knockout clothes.

She told herself that if she changed her look, more people would notice her, would see her with Gabe and believe their engagement.

Who was she kidding? She knew the real reason for wanting to change.

She was already annoyed with him for treating her as if she were a kid while she was having to fight an attraction to him. She'd make him see her as the grown woman she'd become.

After all, wouldn't it serve him right if he had a little fight of his own to deal with?

Three

Late Saturday night after he was home, Gabe sent a brief text asking Meg to go to a dinner dance at the Downly Country Club in honor of its renovation. She sent a return text immediately, accepting his invitation.

He thought about their deal—a month-long fake engagement. Her request had surprised him. But it was her kiss that had stunned him, and from the wide-eyed look he had received, she had been as shocked as he had. He had never expected kissing Meg to be anything except sweet and he had been amused when he'd teased her about it beforehand. He'd expected his request to throw her into a quandary, that they'd have a sweet kiss and that would be all there was to it. He had never envisioned what had actually happened. Maybe he should have guessed because he'd had a sexual reaction to her at the ranch, but he'd never dreamed kissing her would be akin to a nuclear meltdown.

Her searing kiss had shifted their relationship forever. He would never again view her the same way he had before. With that kiss he wanted her in his bed.

His common sense rejected that possibility completely. She was still Meg, still his best friend, still Hank's big sister. She was earnest, sweet, trustworthy, intelligent, and if she had a real relationship he was sure she would be into commitment and marriage. He suspected that had never really happened. They had lost touch through her college years and he didn't know if she'd had boyfriends, but he would bet the ranch there was no guy in her bed on a regular basis at any point in time.

Meg was the type to equate love, kisses and bed with vows, marriage and home.

Regardless, the woman had caused him a sleepless night. She had him all wound up and wanting to hold and kiss her. That reaction still stunned him. He'd never thought about kissing her and never for one second expected any kind of positive reaction on his part. Now Meg's steamy kiss was something he had to deal with in the coming month.

Just remembering her kiss could put him in a sweat. He wanted to pick up the phone and ask her out tomorrow night and seduce her. But that would make him a sneaking, dirty rat who could no longer be called her best friend, and he would feel like the jerk of the year if he didn't propose to her. Neither outcome looked good.

He hadn't imagined what he'd felt and it wasn't because he hadn't been out with a woman in a long time. And it wasn't faulty memory. As impossible as it seemed, Meg was hot and sexy.

He had thought, as sweet as Meg was, this fake engagement might get tedious before a month was over. Now his worries had swung the other way. Now this fake engagement might be too tempting to resist seduction.

He didn't like Justin and was happy to see that she wanted to break off seeing him. But now he could understand why Justin was all for this marriage of convenience.

Gabe groaned. "Damn, how will I get through a month with her?"

He thought he would plan to be out of town on business a lot of the time. A month wasn't long. At least it wasn't long until he thought it would mean thirty nights when he might be with her, kissing her, having to resist temptation. He put his head in his hands.

When he told her he would go along with the fake engagement, he hadn't given a thought to kissing her. Now he couldn't stop thinking about it.

Saturday night he needed to keep a clear head and not do anything he would regret later. He had to keep one thought paramount in his mind: Meg was the marrying kind, and if he ever took her into his bed, he'd have to marry her for real.

And that was the one thing that could never happen.

* * *

After a restless night, the last thing Meg needed was a day with her family. But the next day, after joining her family at church, she took a home-made peach cobbler to her parents' house for Sunday dinner.

As they sat around the dining room table, eating slices of tender roast beef and mashed potatoes with brown gravy, the topic she was loath to hear came up.

"I saw Justin's mother last night and she said he was out of town. If we'd known, you could have gone to dinner with us last night," her mother said.

"Thanks. I ran into an old friend and we went out last night," she said, glancing around the table. Her dad didn't react; he was concentrating on his meal, the gray in his light brown hair shining in the dining room chandelier. He still wore his best brown suit and tie from church. Carlotta Aldridge, her paternal grandmother, sat on his right. Carlotta's short, straight brown-and-gray hair hung just below her ears. She was the grandmother who had spent hours reading to Meg when she had been small. Carlotta wore her favorite color, a frilly pink dress. Next to her was Meg's paternal grandfather, Mason Aldridge, whose thick gray hair was slightly curly above his long, thin face. He had been a rancher all his life and it showed in his weathered brown skin and rough, callused hands. He had taught Meg to ride a horse and take care of her pets.

Seated beside Meg was her maternal grand-mother, Lurline Wills, whose round, jolly face had bright blue eyes and a perpetual smile. Meg and her brothers called her Lolo. Meg's mater-nal grandfather was Harry Wills, another oil and gas man who had worked with her dad most of her life and was as angry and bitter as her dad toward Dirkson Callahan. They were all talk-ing, set to enjoy another delicious Sunday feast, and she was going to end their peaceful Sunday gathering.

"Who's the old friend?" her mother asked, pass-ing hot rolls around the table. "Here's honey. Also raspberry jam," she said, passing small dishes.

"Gabe Callahan and I went out. It was fun to see him again," Meg said, taking a roll and aware all conversation had stopped and the room had gone silent.

"Oh, dear. Megan, we don't speak to the Callahans," Grandma Lurline said, frowning and pushing her glasses up on her nose to stare at Meg. "We haven't spoken to any of those dreadful Callahans for years."

Meg glanced around the table and smiled while everyone else frowned. Both sets of grandparents sat scowling at her. "Gabe and I have always been friends. We had a very good time," Meg said cheerfully. "And we do speak to each other. As a matter of fact, we're going out again next weekend."

Her mother dropped her fork. "Oh, no. Megan, you can't do that."

"Of course I can," Meg replied. "I've got a date with him."

"What about Justin?" her dad asked, his face getting red.

She took a deep breath. "I'm not dating Justin. I'm sorry if spending a little time with Gabe upsets all of you, but I have my friends and Gabe isn't responsible for what his father did or does.

Dirkson Callahan hurt his sons, so don't blame Gabe for his dad's actions. And as for Justin—I've said all along, I am not interested in Justin and he isn't interested in me. We're not getting engaged or married. We're finished."

"Justin and his family think you're serious," her mother said. "Justin has said you are both talking about marriage and making plans. That's what Francis told me."

"That isn't my view because we're not making plans." She picked up her fork and speared a slice of meat. "Mom, you, Grana and Lolo have worked hard fixing a wonderful Sunday dinner. Let's enjoy this delicious roast."

For an instant, all of them stared at her in silence and then her mother smiled. "You're right. We can talk about it later. We did work too hard on this to let it get cold and go uneaten," she said, smiling at the others. The grandmothers nodded as her mother picked up two bowls to pass around the table. "Here are fresh squash and sliced tomatoes from Dad's garden."

Conversation picked up again and Meg relaxed, talking about the dinner and the garden, and avoiding any mention of Gabe or Justin.

It was late afternoon when she got in her car to go home and her mother came rushing out the back door.

"I wanted to talk to you before you go," she said after Meg rolled down her window. "I hope you rethink seeing Gabe Callahan. You know our families don't get along."

"Gabe and I had a good time. We've been friends forever," she said. "I'm going out with him next weekend." Difficult as it was, she faced her mother, realizing the woman had more gray hairs streaked in among the brown hair around her face. Meg felt a pang because she was going to worry her family, but she had to worry them or end up married to a man she didn't love.

"You know what kind of man Gabe Callahan is," her mother said. "Besides being Dirkson Callahan's son, he's got a reputation for being wild and taking risks. He was a terrible influence on Hank. Your father is so unhappy to hear you're going out with him."

Meg smiled at her mother. "I love you and I

love my family with all my heart, but I have to live my life. I had a good time with Gabe and I want to see him again. Sorry, Mom, if no one in my family is happy with me, but I can't date someone to please my family."

She patted her mother on her arm. "I'm not marrying Gabe next weekend. I'm just going out with him. And he moves in the same social circle Justin does. Now stop worrying. It's just an evening with a friend." She gave her mother a smile. "I better head home because I have a busy week ahead. Thanks again. Dinner was wonderful."

Her mother stood waving as she drove away. Meg sighed with relief because she felt another hurdle was over. Her family knew she was going out with Gabe.

Monday afternoon she received a text from Justin saying he wouldn't be in until late Thursday night and asking her to dinner Friday. She declined, telling him she had a benefit to attend with one of her friends. Instead, she made plans to meet him at the café for a quick bite Thursday night. Suspecting he had heard about Gabe, she wanted to make their breakup official then. She was anxious to break the news to him about Gabe and she didn't want to spend an entire evening with Justin to do so.

She hadn't heard a word from Gabe, but she hadn't expected to. This was a favor he was doing for her and there wouldn't be any reason for him to call to talk. She smiled at the thought. He probably wouldn't give a thought to her or his agreement until the end of the week.

Tuesday night Meg sat in her Dallas house and planned Saturday night at the formal country club where she and Gabe would be seen by Justin, his family and her family. She hoped Justin would be there with someone else. He hadn't gotten around to asking her and she was certain he expected her to attend with him. That was, he would until she broke the news to him Thursday night. Meanwhile, she still needed to get a dress for Saturday night, and her makeover.

She smiled in anticipation. Soon she would be free of her family's meddling, thanks to Gabe. Now, if she could just resist his kisses, all would be well. No wonder half the eligible women in the county liked to go out with him.

Thursday afternoon after work when she drove home, she was surprised to see Gabe's black pickup in her driveway. Curious, she parked in her garage, took a glance at herself in the rearview mirror before she got out and smoothed her plaid cotton blouse and faded jeans. She wore scuffed brown boots and she had a navy band holding her hair back from her face—everything about her as plain as ever, she thought. She walked out to find him waiting near the gate that led to the back door. As she looked at him, her pulse jumped. In his black Stetson, jeans, black boots and a Western-style blue cotton shirt, he looked every inch the rancher he was. He also was handsome enough to be a celebrity. Slight dark stubble shaded his jaw, giving him a rugged touch that added to his appeal. How could she have gone all those years without noticing how handsome he was? He took her breath away now just standing still and doing nothing. And the closer she got, the better she could see the fantastic, thickly lashed blue eyes that made her heart beat faster.

Another phenomenon that shocked her. Those blue eyes she had looked into all her life could make her heart race now. Go figure that one. She shook her head without realizing what she was doing.

"Why are you shaking your head at me? Would you rather I get in my truck and go? What am I doing wrong?" he asked as she stopped in front of him.

"You're doing nothing wrong. It's just that you're the same as ever and at the same time, you're not," she said, unable to stop herself from revealing her thoughts. "Maybe I just never really noticed you. You have sinfully wicked blue eyes." She was still shocked over his kiss and her reaction, and she couldn't keep from telling him what she noticed now about him because she liked him and was struggling with the attraction.

He grinned and placed his hands on his hips. "You're putting me on to try to get me to be convincing in this little scheme of yours. You don't have to do that. I'll take you out where we'll be seen and let you stay at my ranch. I've already agreed, so stop trying to pour it on and schmooze me into this fake love."

"You fantastic man," she gushed, amused how he had taken her remark. "I'm going to make you miss me when I'm out of your life again."

He stepped closer to place his hands lightly on her shoulders, and she was instantly aware of his touch, his proximity and her heart beating faster. "You're not going out of my life. That will never happen as long as we're both alive and well. I'm sure you're doing all of this just in case anyone is watching. Let's go inside and you can be yourself."

"Sure. What brings you to my house?" she asked him as she dug in her purse for her keys.

"I was in Dallas, so I decided to stop by and see you and catch up on where you stand with Justin."

"I turned down an invitation to go out with him Friday night. I have a charity event to attend with a friend, so it's no lie. He gets back into town tonight and I told him I would meet him for a bite.

I'm driving myself so I can leave. It isn't a date. This is goodbye."

"I take it your friend is female and not someone else who could have done this fake engagement."

"She is female, and no one else could have done this except you. You're perfect. I told you that. I don't think you pay attention to me sometimes," she said.

"Darlin', since we kissed, you get so much of my attention you wouldn't believe it if I told you."

Stopping abruptly, she tilted her head and smiled at him. "Do I really? That's exciting to hear."

"Maybe. I didn't much think you wanted any real attraction to spring up between us."

Her smile vanished. "You sure know how to kill happy moments." She pulled out her key. "Come in and we can have a drink and I'll give you the tour."

"Yeah, give me the tour. It might come in handy if I can describe your bedroom, or at least sound as if I have an inkling of what it looks like."

She laughed. "I'll give you the tour, but you're not going to have to tell anyone about my bedroom and I doubt if you do that with anyone else you're with." She was aware of him at her side, his height and long stride. Had one kiss created this instant, intense awareness of Gabe that she'd never had before in her life?

"Of course I don't, but Justin might just suspect you of doing exactly what you are doing— faking an engagement."

"Oh, no, he won't," she declared. "Not when he hears Tanya's and Cassie's reports on last weekend. We looked convincing, I'm sure. And then your reputation—at least as far as seduction is concerned—will convince him easily," she said, thinking about all the reasons she had gone over several times in her mind. "Now, the fact that you are engaged to me will be a little more difficult to sell, but that's where my lifetime of being frank and honest to a fault will carry us through this."

He shook his head. "You've got this all figured out and I have to admit, you're right."

"Just wait until that ring is on my finger and I've been to the wedding store in Downly. There won't be a doubting soul in town," she said, thinking more about Gabe brushing against her lightly as they entered the kitchen. As he hung his hat on a rack by the door next to two of her hats, her gaze ran across his broad shoulders and down to his narrow waist. It took an effort to pay attention to what he was saying.

"Don't get me roped into showers and having to return presents later. Also, I want to tell my brothers the truth. They'll laugh and forget it. I don't want them planning anything for us or getting some lavish wedding gifts. Ditto my mom, although if I didn't let her in on this, I don't think she'd believe it until she received an invitation to a rehearsal dinner, and we're not going that far."

"No, we're not. Your mom wouldn't believe it?"

"I doubt it, but I want to let her know the truth from the start."

"Sure. Let your family know. I'm sorry to be deceitful with my family. I never have been, but they've pushed me into this. I'm desperate. Mom is looking at wedding cakes and showing me pictures. Yuk." She put down her purse and the papers she'd carried in from a job she was designing.

"At least my family knows I'm going out with

you and will continue to do so," she told him. "That's a death knell for a serious relationship with Justin. I expect to tell him farewell the first minute we talk."

"And you think he'll just drift away without trying to convince you otherwise? I don't think so, Meg."

"That's why I want to move into your Dallas house. That will do it. He has strong feelings about a woman being faithful."

Gabe laughed and draped his arm casually across her shoulders. His touch made her tingle and she was intensely aware of him so close beside her. "I would have sworn you didn't have a devious bone in your body until this deal. My, oh, my, how I misjudged you," he said, looking down at her. "I misjudged you in other ways, too," he said, suddenly turning serious, and his solemn gaze made her pulse jump.

"I don't think I want to pursue what other ways," she said breathlessly, aware how close he stood and thinking about his kiss. The moment stretched and she realized how they were staring at each other.

"Last Sunday, dinner at my parents' house was grim for a little while. Mom was on my case. Dad looked as if he could eat nails. My grandparents were all horrified because you know how they feel about your dad."

"I hate it when people think I'm just like my father," Gabe said and lowered his arm, propping his hands on his hips. "Just because he ran roughshod over people and his family, that doesn't mean I do."

She patted his hand, a spontaneous reaction that she had done lots of times in the past, except now, tingles radiated from the casual contact and she yanked her hand away as if burned.

Gabe didn't seem to notice and she guessed he was lost in thoughts about his father.

"Do you want something to drink? Iced tea, cold beer—"

"Yes, I want something," he said in a husky voice that took her breath away.

Her heart skipped again. How had a kiss changed their whole relationship?

"A drink, Gabe. Do you want iced tea, cold beer—"

"You said the magic words—cold beer."

"Coming right up," she said as she went into the kitchen.

When she turned from the fridge, she was surprised to see him right in front of her. Her gaze ran over him, reminding her of standing in his embrace while he kissed her. She cleared her throat before she could speak. "Why don't you get cookies out of the cookie jar on the counter or get some pretzels from the cabinet while I get my juice." Truthfully, she just wanted to put some distance between them.

He rummaged in a cabinet and got a sack of pretzels while she poured her grape juice over ice.

"Come on and have a quick tour and we'll sit on the patio and talk. It's shaded from the sun after three or four and it's bearable. We have a breeze today."

He took a sip of beer and set the bottle on the table to follow her into the adjoining living area and he glanced around. He seemed to fill the small room and her gaze ran over him again. "I'm surprised that you like contemporary furniture.

I figured you for the fancy, old-fashioned furniture you grew up with."

"This room is what I prefer, but I have both because Mom gave me my bedroom furniture."

He smiled. "I know what that looks like then. The big four-poster mahogany bed," he said walking around the living room and looking through an open door. "I'm right. There it is," he said. "Hey…" He disappeared through the door into a narrow hallway and she followed, curious why he went to look at something.

The minute she stepped into her room, she regretted not checking things over before she offered a tour. Gabe crossed the room to the bed and picked up the little brown teddy bear he had given her so many years ago.

He turned to look at her. "Is my memory right? Why have you hung on to this all these years? Or is it out here for Justin's benefit?"

"No, it is not for Justin's benefit, because Justin doesn't get invited into this room. I just thought I might need it so I got it out of the closet."

Gabe laughed and tossed it back on the bed. He crossed the room to her to put his hands on her shoulders again and his blue eyes twinkled with devilment. "So Justin has never gotten into your bedroom, but he expects to marry you? I've forgotten how old-fashioned you can be. Justin is probably being and doing whatever you want to get a ring on your finger."

"I told you that we're both being pushed by our families."

Gabe laughed and shook his head. "I'm ready to sit and drink my beer. I've seen enough to indicate that I know my way around the place." He started out of the room and she walked with him, stepping through the door ahead of him.

"I forget that sometimes you can be annoying."

"But you still love me, don't you? You even still want to be engaged to me," he said, laughing as he teased her. "You need me, so you can't really get mad at me," he said, draping his arm casually across her shoulders. Only his touch wasn't casual to her. She had a prickly awareness of him and a sudden vivid recollection of his kiss.

As if he knew her thoughts, he turned her to face him. "We could have a lot more fun if we spend our time kissing."

"Will you stop?" she said. "We don't have an audience, therefore there is no point in kissing."

"*Au contraire*, my darlin'," he said. He laughed and threw up his hands, walking away. "I can see my teasing is getting to you. We'll go sit, make plans while I drink my beer and then I'll go home."

"That's better."

Holding his beer and the pretzels in one hand, he draped his arm around her shoulders. "This is great, to renew our friendship. I'd forgotten how much I liked having you for a friend. And now that we're kissin' friends, I *really* like having you for a friend." They stepped out on her shaded patio and he held a black metal chair for her. After she sat, he pulled a chair beside her, sat and propped his booted feet on a low iron table in front of him. "So you'll tell Justin good-bye tonight and Saturday night you'll go out with me. Right?"

"Correct. Tonight I expect to break it off with him for good."

"Should I gulp down my beer and go? Am I keeping you from getting ready?"

"Heavens, no. It's only four in the afternoon and I don't see him until eight."

"I figured you'd be getting yourself all—"

"If you say 'beautiful,' I'm going to take your beer away from you and send you home now."

He smiled at her. "I can't resist getting you all hot and bothered. You always rise to the bait." He chuckled and sipped his beer.

"Hot and bothered, huh?" she said, half amused and half annoyed with him because sometimes he still treated her the same way he did when they were kids. She set down her drink and turned to face him. "I'll show you hot and bothered," she said. She stood, swung her leg across his and sat in his lap, wrapping her arms around his neck and kissing him on the mouth.

She poured herself into her kiss, wanting to get back at him for all his teasing and give him something to think about before he teased her again.

For an instant she assumed he was startled, but then his arms circled her tightly and he kissed her in return. A passionate kiss that made her forget teasing and realize she might have set herself up for something more worrisome. She had wanted to set him on fire with her kiss, to make him see her as a woman and not the kid next door he could tease and torment and still be friends with. Too late, she realized she might have stirred up a bushel of trouble for herself.

She felt his arousal press against her and her heart raced while she, too, burned with desire. She was shaking with wanting him, hot with the need for more.

Remembering what had started their kiss, she stopped as abruptly as she'd begun. They stared at each other and then she moved off his lap and walked away. "That got out of hand," she whispered, not sure whether he heard her and not really caring because she spoke the words more to herself than him. Despite what she'd said, she wanted to turn around, go back to him and continue where she'd left off. And that scared her.

"On that note, I better take my cue and get the hell out of here before I try to carry you off to that four-poster bed," he said. "I'll call you, Meg. I know my way out."

She merely nodded. "Bye, Gabe."

She heard the back door close and walked to

the window to watch him get into his pickup and back out down her drive. In seconds he was gone.

She touched her lips. She wanted him so badly, she wasn't going to be able to resist him. Suddenly she realized something: he hadn't been flirting this afternoon. Gabe had been teasing her, the way her brothers would have teased her. He didn't really see her as a woman like the women he dated.

She placed her hands on her hips in an indignant pose. She'd show him she was a woman. Saturday night. Silently she thanked her friend Barb, who'd told her about a fabulous makeover she'd had when she had been hired for a commercial. Barb had set up her appointment in a Dallas salon for Saturday.

Tomorrow, she would rearrange her schedule so she could shop for a dress. One way or another, she'd make Gabe see her for what she was: a grown-up, desirable woman.

At the same time, common sense told her to leave the situation as it was. As long as he saw her the way he always had, she would be less appealing to him and he would be less so to her. She never wanted to fall in love with him anyway, so why get a makeover and attract his attention? On the other hand, he might forever see her as a kid and she didn't want that, either.

Unfortunately, she had no such problem seeing him for what he was. Gabe had grown into a handsome, sexy man who would carry her off to his bed and steal her heart away if she wasn't careful. To her, he was no longer the kid from her past, the boy next door, a fun friend she could trust, just Gabe, friendly, nice. Never in the past had he made her heart beat like crazy or her insides turn to jelly or the room suddenly too hot to bear. Back then she hadn't seen him as the most handsome man she knew. She hadn't wanted his arms around her and his mouth on hers.

She did now. And it wasn't good.

Common sense told her to cancel the makeover, and she got out her phone. She should let well enough alone. Get loose from Justin, tell Gabe thank you and go on her way, forgetting Gabe as she had for the past ten or eleven years.

That was the sensible approach.

Then she thought about Saturday night. At the

country club it would be a formal dinner. Gabe would be in a tux and look handsome and she would look just like she did for her first-grade Christmas party, wearing the same hairstyle and type of dress. And she knew she couldn't do it. She was a woman and she wanted him to see her as one.

As foolish as it was, it was a risk she was willing to take. She knew what she had to do.

She put her phone away.

At eight o'clock she sat in a booth in the small casual sandwich shop and watched Justin come up the walk. She had come early and wanted to be waiting when he arrived. Slightly taller than Gabe, he was handsome by any standard with thick brown hair and thickly lashed pale brown eyes. His prominent cheekbones and straight nose added to his good looks. She guessed he was probably at least an inch taller than Gabe. Both men were broad-shouldered, but Gabe was definitely more muscular. In a charcoal suit, white dress shirt and red tie, Justin looked handsome, successful and filled with energy. He had come directly from the airport. Justin had dated other women in his social circle who were beautiful and probably in love with him, and Meg would never understand why this marriage of convenience appealed to him except for family pressures. He had been engaged once to another woman whose family moved in his social circle and Justin had been the one who had broken it off. He had talked about the breakup with her, explaining that he hadn't known whether he could really trust his ex-fiancée to be faithful, and that he had to have that in a wife. Meg had listened to him talk, wondering what he was leaving out, because his reasoning had had some gaps, but she hadn't quizzed him about it. She knew Justin had women who would have his parents' approval who wanted to go out with him, so this crazy pressure for them to marry made no sense to her. Granted, Tanya wasn't one of those women, but from the little things Justin had said, she suspected he truly loved Tanya.

Justin kissed her forehead and they exchanged pleasantries before he got to the point.

"I might as well explain why I wanted to see

you tonight. I heard you went out Saturday night with Gabe Callahan."

"Yes, I did. You and I have no commitment."

"We're on the verge of one," he said, frowning. "A huge commitment."

"I've told you I'm not interested in a commitment. I don't want a marriage of convenience. Gabe and I have been friends since I was three. We went out last weekend and had fun talking about old times. I have a date with him Saturday night to the country club dedication of the new ballroom."

Justin leaned across the table. "Break the date with Callahan. It will be unpleasant for everyone if you don't. Our parents and your grandparents will be there."

They paused when a waiter came to take their orders and as soon as he left, Justin leaned forward again. "I intended us to go together," he added.

"You didn't ask me," she said. Justin wore a scowl and his jaw was clamped shut. She knew he was angry, but her peace of mind and her freedom were at stake so she had to end this.

"I've accepted Gabe's invitation and I'm going with him. I'm not ready for a commitment to you. No one has listened to me. Not you, not my parents and not yours."

"Dammit, Megan. You're ruining everything. You're throwing away a future to go out with a wild, party-loving cowboy who will toss you aside in no time."

Their waiter came and Justin became silent while their drinks were placed on the table with their sandwiches.

"You're tossing aside all plans of us marrying, aren't you?" he asked.

"Yes, I am. We're not in love."

"Our parents want us to marry. We fit together. We're the same social circle, the same background. It would be perfect. You know I want a political career and you would be an asset."

"Thank you, Justin. But you'll be happier if you marry someone you love, a person you're thrilled to be with and you can't wait to come home to."

"I've been honest with you and I've told you what I want and what my family wants. I've told you what's in it for us and it's a lot of money and opportunities. My dad wants us to marry and he wants a grandchild. I'll get a partnership in the firm after you and I are married a year."

She studied Justin while he talked and her gratitude to Gabe for the fake engagement soared with every word.

"I'm so sorry to cut you out of a partnership, but you could go to work for someone besides your father. You're sharp and a good, successful attorney who will do well wherever you are. You don't have to work for your dad to be successful."

"I'll move up faster with my dad."

She could see she was getting nowhere with him. Hurtful as it might be, she had to be frank. "Justin, I'm going out with Gabe Callahan. You and I are finished even discussing this." She fumbled for her wallet. "I'll buy the dinners—"

"Dammit, Megan. I'll get our damn sandwiches. You're making a big mistake. You keep dating Gabe Callahan and we're through," he said.

"I understand that," she answered and his face flushed. She stood and he came to his feet, too. "Goodbye, Justin, and good luck."

"Gabe Callahan will not marry you, so don't count on that. He's not marrying anyone."

"I know that."

She turned and was out the door in seconds. She took a deep breath as she hurried to her car, eager to get away. She was finally free of Justin. She wanted to grab Gabe and hug him for being the catalyst that got her out of the sticky situation.

Once she got home, she went to her bedroom, grabbed the brown teddy bear and danced around her room with it. "I'm free."

Saturday night she would get engaged to Gabe, a silly fake engagement, but it would be exactly what she needed to make this breakup last. Up till now her life had been filled with doing what other people wanted her to do. From now on, she'd do what she wanted to do for herself. Starting with her makeover. And then she'd get engaged to Gabe and move into his house.

It was finally happening. Living her own life.

Amid her elation, she had one disturbing thought: Could she really do it? Live under the same roof with Gabe without ending up in bed with him?

Four

Gabe tried to keep his mind on business the next day, but it was difficult. He kept thinking about Meg, remembering when she had suddenly straddled him, sat on his lap and kissed him. The kiss had made him feel as if he would burst into flames, had set his heart pounding so hard he'd thought she could hear each beat.

He couldn't resist teasing her sometimes, because it was fun and because he knew it annoyed her. But she did the same thing back to him in her own way. She kissed him until he lost all rational thought.

How did she do that?

All he knew was that he wanted her in his bed, but each time he thought that, his conscience tore at him. She was his childhood best friend who trusted him completely and she had come to him for help, not for seduction. He could not seduce her.

"Damn," he said aloud. From the minute she told him what she wanted, he had known she was going to drag him into trouble with her plea for a fake engagement. And it was only going to get worse, because this weekend she was moving in with him.

He dreaded all of it. He wouldn't back out of his agreement to help, despite the fact that she complicated his life more with each passing minute. And if he wasn't careful, he might end up with a real engagement instead of a fake one, and he was not ready for that.

"Damn," Gabe said again, shaking his head.

He couldn't wait for tomorrow night at the country club. Justin's parents and Meg's parents would be there. He'd be relieved when that evening was over because it ought to finish Justin's dream of a marriage of convenience. Did he ever pick the wrong woman to try to push or bribe into a loveless marriage.

Gabe grabbed his hat and left to throw himself into working with his men on moving cattle from one pasture to another.

Meg took a few hours off work Friday to shop for a new dress and shoes for Saturday night's formal dinner dance. She found a sleeveless black crepe dress with a deep-vee neckline, a straight, ankle-length skirt and a high slit on one side. She paired it with stiletto-heeled black sandals.

On Saturday she had her makeover. It took all day, but that night while she waited for Gabe, she stared at herself in the mirror and couldn't believe what she saw.

She twirled in front of her full-length mirror and smiled. She barely recognized herself and she hoped Gabe wouldn't recognize her at all.

Gabe rang Meg's doorbell and as he waited, he gave himself a pep talk. That morning, somewhere between feeding the stock and mending a fence, he'd come to a realization. One he'd reiterated to himself again and again. Meg was just Meg—a childhood chum and now a friend he intended to help before going on his way. During the normal course of life these days, they rarely even saw each other. He'd simply missed her in his life—that's why she suddenly seemed so attractive. It wasn't the hot kisses, he told himself. Meg was filled with life and he was glad to be back with her. And this was just a temporary situation that would be over in three weeks.

Reinforced by his thoughts, he punched the doorbell again. What was she doing?

The door swung open and he was startled. For one brief moment he thought he had the wrong house. His gaze raked over a very tall stunning blonde, her silky hair falling to her shoulders in spiral curls. Her stylish black dress emphasized her creamy skin and luscious long hair while the vee neckline revealed full curves that made his temperature soar. She had a tiny waist and long legs with shoes that gave her additional height.

"I'm sor—" He stopped and peered at the woman while his pulse pounded and the world grew warmer.

"Meg?" he said, for once in his adult life feeling like an awkward teen with a new date—a feeling that he had rarely experienced even as a teen. "Meg?" he repeated, unable to believe he faced her. Shocked, he could only stare.

She smiled, a smile that lit up her perfectly made-up face.

"Why don't you come inside, Gabe." She stepped back, took his arm and drew him inside. He merely followed, unable to take his eyes off her, unable to speak.

"You look very handsome in your black tux. Sophisticated and wealthy and elegant."

Again, he remained silent. He was absolutely flummoxed by the sight of her.

"We'll go inside until you're finished looking at me," she said, sounding amused. "From your expression, I take it you like what you see?" When he didn't reply, she walked into the living room.

He followed her, captivated by the slight sway of her hips, the clinging ankle-length skirt, the glimpse of a long leg through the slit in the side of it. He inhaled her intoxicating perfume, a brand that was definitely not lilac scented.

When he'd taken in every inch of her, he slowly came out of his shocked stupor. He tried to collect his wits and act like a normal guy ready to go out for the evening. But it wasn't easy when his brain could form only one thought: *Wow!*

When she crossed in front of him, he caught her arm lightly and turned her to face him, then placed his hands on her hips, feeling as if he faced a stranger. He could feel her warm body and her soft curves, the silky material of her dress beneath his hands.

"You're stunning. You look gorgeous," he said in a raspy voice.

"Thank you. I'm glad you noticed and like the change."

"I'd have to be blind or dead not to notice or like how you look. You take my breath away." Suddenly, he could feel himself sinking even deeper into a quicksand of complications in his life. He had never expected to take out a stunning blonde who could kiss him into a raging fire. This pretend engagement was going to require every ounce of his willpower to keep him from trying to seduce her. He didn't want to take her to the club tonight. Right now, he wanted to take her to bed.

He inhaled deeply. "Oh, darlin', the single guys are going to want to take you home tonight, and this is not the way to get rid of Justin. He won't want to give you up now, even if it becomes a life-or-death fight with me."

She laughed softly. Where did Meg get the soft, seductive laugh? She'd made a total transformation and for one single second he wondered if someone else was trying to pass herself off as Meg tonight. "Are you really Meg?"

"I'm really Meg," she replied, sounding more like herself. He felt tied in knots. He was still in shock from the neck up, his brain unable to process the change in her, but from the waist down he was hot, aroused and ready to pull her into his arms and kiss her until they made love.

"I guarantee you, after Justin sees you tonight this is going to be a battle."

Her smile faded and her brow furrowed as worry clouded her big brown eyes that were now thickly lashed, lined and lidded with a smoky hue. Her makeup was flawless, as if she had come straight from making a movie.

The worried expression didn't last. She drew herself up slightly and smiled, a smile that kept him aroused, aching to make love and still unable to believe his eyes.

"Gabe, if you're worried about Justin and his reaction, I can get someone else to take me. I do have some other guys who are friends."

"I'll bet you do. No, I'll take you, Meg. I just think you've made a move here that will keep Justin trying his damnedest to marry you. I don't think it will be simply a marriage of convenience he's after once he sees you looking like this."

She smiled. "You're sweet. I have two big bags and a carry-on packed—one bag to take to your ranch and the other bag to take to your Dallas house. I'm still going home with you tonight, right?" she asked with an air of great innocence.

"Damn right, you're going home with me. Oh, yeah," he said, wondering if he would be able to resist her once he got her there alone.

"Then we'll get my bags now," she prompted.

"Sure," he said. But he stood there, lost in thought about taking her home with him.

She laughed. "Gabe? My bags?"

"Oh, sure. I'll get them now and we'll get going," he said, coming out of his stupor. "Unless you'll let me kiss you a few times first."

She laughed and shook her head.

"Not on your life. You would mess up my makeup and probably my dress. We're going to the club now."

"It's going to be an effort to stop looking at you long enough to drive. You really are stunning."

"Thank you," she said, and he wondered if she was making fun of him. He didn't care. He could hardly stop looking at her. How had he known her all his life and not seen how gorgeous she really was?

He carried out her bags and then returned for her. "Let's go," he said, taking her arm.

As they stepped outside she frowned. "Oh, you've taken your sports car."

He grinned. "Half the world drools when they see this car. You look as if you want to run and get your pickup."

"I've gotten more nervous about speed and risks since Hank was killed. Do me a favor and keep it at the speed limit or lower."

"Sure," he said, smiling and shaking his head. "I might as well have brought my old car. Okay. We'll go slowly because I don't want a white-knuckled passenger. You didn't used to be this way."

"I used to have Hank."

"Sorry, Meg," Gabe said, hugging her lightly. "I miss him, too. But you know, he wasn't as wild as you think."

"Yes, he was. You don't know the difference because you're the same way."

"Are we having an argument at the beginning of the evening?"

She flashed a radiant smile that felt like a blast of sunshine. "Absolutely not. I think you're a wonderful driver and I can't wait to ride with you, my handsome prince to the rescue."

"This prince can't wait to kiss his princess good-night at the end of the evening."

"I'll try not to disappoint you," she whispered.

"I'd be willing to bet every cent I own that you will not disappoint me at all."

She smiled. "We'll see."

He could only stare at her full, stunning red lips. Her eyes might be gorgeous but her mouth was pure temptation. Damn, he was getting hotter by the second.

His voice was husky when he finally spoke. "I'm about ready to go back inside now and get some of those kisses."

"Oh, no," she said, not a bit rattled. "I want Justin and my family to see us."

"Absolutely. And I'll be drooling over you all evening."

"Frankly, I hope not," she said and they both laughed.

Once they were on their way, he made an effort to keep the sports car well below the speed limit and his attention firmly on his driving, even though he'd have preferred to just sit and look at her. How could she have changed that much from just makeup and hair color? Part of it was also the dress, he admitted. He had never seen her in a sexy dress like the one she was wearing tonight.

"Your parents and Justin's are still coming to-night, right?"

"Oh, yes. And both sets of my grandparents. Justin has a table reserved with friends so he's going to have to explain why I'm not with him, which is good. You know he's listed as one of the twenty most desirable bachelors in the Dallas area. And so are you, for that matter."

He shrugged. "I don't know why the hell I'm in there. I'm a cowboy. I don't give a damn about these country clubs. I only belong to this club because of family and because it's convenient sometimes since it's in Dallas and near the area where I live. I shouldn't be on that list."

"Of course you should," she said, rubbing his knee lightly, her voice a sultry drawl. "You fantastic man—you are *sooo* sexy and handsome."

He knew she was teasing and he glanced her way to give her a smile. He had to drag his eyes back to the road. Three days ago he would have laughed, paid no attention to her and gone on to some other topic. Right now, he was breaking into a sweat, on fire and thinking of getting her into bed. She sounded like the same ol' Meg, but she didn't look the same and it made a boatload of difference.

"We'll sit with my family—not my parents, of course," he said, trying to get his thoughts on their conversation and off erotic images of them scorching the sheets. "My dad lives out of the country and my mom is out of the country with friends now. We'll be with my half brother, Blake, and his wife, Sierra. And my brother Cade and his wife, Erin."

"I don't know Blake very well. He wasn't around those years you and I saw a lot of each other."

"My half brother and I have different mothers and those mothers didn't get along. Cade and Blake became friends in high school and Cade pulled him into the family—at least as far as the brothers are concerned."

"I've met Blake, but not his wife."

"Sierra is great. You'll see. And so is Cade's wife, Erin. When Nathan and his wife were killed in the car wreck, Cade became their little girl's guardian. Amelia is a doll." Cade had stepped up big-time at a dark hour when the family had been devastated by a drunk driver. Gabe had a lot of respect for his brother.

"Blake and Sierra have a little girl, too," he explained. "Emily, born in January. The kids won't be there tonight, but you'll get to meet them at some point." He glanced her way and saw a sadness overtake her face. No doubt, talking about his late brother reminded her of her own lost sibling. He quickly changed the subject. "I can't wait to see your parents go into shock when they see you."

"I went by their place before I went home to dress. They know I'm a blonde now. And they know I'm going with you."

He scoffed. "I can imagine the reception I'll get."

"Well, you've lived with that attitude since your dad bought mine out. My family hasn't spoken to you or any Callahan in years and tonight won't be an exception."

"No doubt you'll be hearing from Justin tonight. I wouldn't be surprised if he shows up on your doorstep."

"I'm not going home tonight, remember? I'm

going home with you. My moving in with you should put an end to Justin."

Gabe grinned. "Justin is burned toast. I hope he realizes it."

Minutes later, as they approached the club where valets waited, Gabe slowed the car and glanced at her. "Here's your last chance. I can still drive out of here and take you home. I guarantee you when Justin sees you tonight, he isn't going to want to give you up. He'll want to marry you more than ever. A whole lot more than ever."

"Don't be silly. I'm still me. I don't look that different."

"Oh, yes, you do. For a while, I didn't recognize you. I promise you the 'new you' will change how Justin feels about you."

"That's exciting to hear. Maybe I should act sexier," she said in a sultry drawl. "That way I won't seem like such a kid to you. Has my new appearance changed how you feel about me?"

He pulled the car over to the side of the road, so other vehicles could pass them, and turned to her. As he wound his fingers in her hair that was now so soft and silky, he looked at her wide-eyed expression.

"Meg, I'm trying to be your friend, like a brother to you. Don't push the sexy come-on tonight unless you want to face the consequences. Kissing you is fantastic and I'm no saint. I can only resist so much. The way you look now makes me forget completely the relationship we've always had. Be careful what you get yourself into, unless that's really what you want."

This close, he felt her sweet breath on his face and all he wanted to do was lean in and kiss her. That and peel her out of that enticing black dress.

"Okay," she said. "Friends forever. I get it. Don't worry. In a little while I'll look like my old self again."

Reluctantly Gabe released her and turned to drive up to the valet.

"I can feel my freedom already. I'm so happy, Gabe. Thank you again."

"You can show me your appreciation when we get back to my place tonight," he said, smiling at her, and she laughed. Taking a deep breath, he tried to relax and get back to their familiar relationship, but he suspected that wasn't going to happen again in their lifetimes. There was no way to forget how she looked tonight. Or how she could kiss.

He couldn't wait for the evening to end. He had looked forward to seeing his brothers and their wives, but now he wanted to have Meg all to himself, which surprised him.

Everything about her surprised him now.

He got out of the car and walked around it while a valet held the door for her and she stepped out. She was poised, radiant and absolutely breath-taking. He couldn't stop looking at her. Her new appearance pushed him into more complications, yet now he looked forward to spending time with her this evening, not his family.

The event schedule was a cocktail hour, dinner, some speeches and then dancing, and he intended to enjoy every minute with her.

He took her arm and they entered the club, turning toward the refurbished ballroom where piano music could be heard. They didn't get far before they encountered Justin and his date.

Meg had turned to speak to someone nearby

while Justin addressed Gabe. Justin started to look away when Meg turned and said hello to him, and Gabe saw the man's jaw drop. He recovered swiftly, his gaze sweeping over her once more, and Gabe couldn't resist slipping his arm around her waist—getting a look from Justin that expressed unmistakable hatred and anger.

"If looks could kill, I would be a dead man now," Gabe said when they walked on.

"Good. I told you we would be taken seriously. Wait until my parents see us. You just keep your arm around me."

"I don't think so. Some things I don't do around parents, and you have very nice parents. I don't want to anger them more than I have to. They don't like me to begin with. I'm still my father's son whether he ever sees me or not."

"Don't worry," she replied, "my family will be civil toward you. And me. This is, after all, a social event."

"Justin's another story. I saw the look on his face."

"Wait until this weekend is over. We will have a

whirlwind courtship and then get engaged. Gabe, I don't know what I'd do without you."

"You keep that thought in your pretty head until we get home."

Why was he flirting with her, while common sense told him to back off? The lady was not his type and he didn't want to get seriously entangled with her. If only he could remember that each time he looked at her. Well, he'd better cling to wisdom like a lifeline when he kissed her tonight. At the mere thought, another heat wave swamped him.

If he had good sense, he wouldn't kiss her—tonight or ever again. But they had a deal. Besides, kisses he couldn't resist. Where he had to use willpower was ensuring they didn't go beyond kissing. He simply had to keep his wits about him.

He laughed to himself. He never would have thought Meg could do anything to make him lose all common sense.

Till now.

They stopped at the table with her parents and grandparents. Meg's dad came to his feet, as well as her grandfather who was the rancher, but her other grandfather did not.

Gabe offered his hand and Meg's father shook it, surprising him. "Hello, Mr. Aldridge, Mrs. Aldridge," he said, smiling at her mother.

Mason Aldridge also shook hands with Gabe, talking briefly to him about livestock and the need for rain.

When the old man sat down, Meg's father leaned in close and said in a harsh, low voice, so only Gabe could hear, "Do not hurt my daughter."

"Yes, sir," Gabe answered quietly. "I never have and I don't plan to. She's been my best friend since before we started school."

"You're a grown man now, not a kid, and she's a beautiful young woman. Don't hurt her."

"No, sir, I won't," he reiterated politely and turned to smile at Meg's mother, who was seated and ignoring him while talking to her mother, who sat beside her.

"We'll see you later," Meg said as she took Gabe's arm and pulled slightly. He didn't need any urging to walk away from her family.

"You get along with my grandfather."

"We're both ranchers. We have some of the same problems. But your dad threatened me. He told me not to hurt you."

"Did he really? I suppose it just never got through to them that they were hurting me by trying to push me into marrying a guy I don't love. By the way, do your brothers know about the fake engagement?"

"Yes, they do, and so do their wives. They accepted it as a simple favor I'm doing. Cade's amused that I would even agree to a fake engagement. And they're worried having a brief engagement may complicate my life."

She frowned. "I hadn't thought about afterward. There may be some women who'll be bothered about a previous engagement. Tell them it wasn't real. I'll be glad to tell anyone."

He smiled. "Don't worry. It won't matter, because marriage is not even remotely on my horizon."

She squeezed his arm lightly. "Well, I'm here if you need me. That's what friends are for."

He needed to remember that friendship when they got back to his house tonight and he was alone with her. He thought about her father's warning to not hurt her. He wasn't worried about her father, but he didn't want to hurt Meg. He glanced around at her, looking at the deep-vee neckline of her dress and how it clung to her lush curves and creamy skin. He was going to have to keep remembering she was his friend, not a lover.

The Callahan brothers stood as Meg and Gabe approached their table. She caught the look that passed between them when they realized who she was.

"Wow, Meg," Cade said, smiling at her, "you don't look like the kid who used to climb over our fence to play ball with us."

She laughed. "Thanks, Cade."

"You may remember Erin, Luke Dorsey's younger sister," Cade said, introducing his wife. "Erin, this is Meg Aldridge, who was our Downly neighbor when Gabe and Meg were growing up."

"We do know each other, although we haven't seen each other in a long time," Meg said, smiling at Erin and remembering her big green eyes and red hair. Gabe touched her back to draw her attention. "Meg, you remember my older brother Blake, and this is his wife, Sierra."

She greeted the other brother and the beautiful brunette.

Gabe pulled out a chair for Meg and she sat at the table with the Callahans. In no time the men were sharing pictures of their babies on their phones. She saw pictures of Amelia, who had been adopted by Cade and Erin, and Sierra and Blake's baby girl, Emily. They seemed so happily married, she couldn't help wondering why Gabe was so opposed to settling down. Tonight wasn't a typical evening for Gabe and he probably wouldn't have attended if he hadn't been doing a favor for her. She knew he liked a wilder time than he was having at the staid country club.

She was grateful to Gabe for pouring on the charm, especially when she could see Justin sitting only a few tables away.

Gabe put his arm lightly across her shoulders and leaned closer. "I see one of my friends. Remember Marc Medina?"

"Yes, I do. I haven't seen him in a long time."

"He isn't going to recognize you. Let's go over and say hello."

Gabe stood and pulled out her chair and then took her hand in his as they wound through tables. Marc saw him coming and stepped away from his table to meet them. She looked at a handsome, broad-shouldered man with thick, wavy hair as black as Gabe's.

"Good to see you," he said to Gabe, shaking hands with him.

"Hey, Marc. Good to see you, too," Gabe said. "You remember Megan."

"Megan, I haven't seen you in a long time. You've grown up into a very beautiful woman," Marc said.

"Thank you."

"I've seen your landscaping around town. It's good. Do you have a card?"

She dug one out of her evening bag and handed it to him.

"Thanks."

"We've got to get back to the family," Gabe said. "We'll get lunch soon. I'll call you."

As they walked away, Gabe said, "Marc is

doing well with his oil and gas business. I'm glad because he's a hardworking guy."

"A nice guy, too, as I recall."

Gabe pulled out her chair and they joined his family again.

With constant attention from Gabe, she couldn't keep from having a wonderful time. After the speeches ended and dinner finished, the band took over, playing soft ballads. She knew from other events that the music would change later in the evening when the older crowd disappeared.

Gabe sat with his arm on the back of her chair, turned slightly to face her. He leaned in close, and to anyone watching them he'd look as if he couldn't take his gaze from her.

"Justin hasn't taken his eyes off you," he whispered. "If I take you out on that dance floor, he'll ask you to dance in a flash."

"I don't think so. I think he'd be afraid I'd say no and embarrass him." She looked up at Gabe, smiling at him. "If he's watching, I hope I look in love."

"Meg, darlin', if the way you look at me gets

any hotter, I'll want to check us into that hotel across the road."

She wiggled with joy as her smile widened. "Oh, that makes my heart really flutter. I want to look so in love with you, no one will have a shred of doubt when we announce this engagement."

He wrapped his arm around her shoulders and pulled her close, nuzzling her neck. Gabe was everything she needed to pull this off. He was charming, fun and sexy, and she wondered how she would get through the month without falling in love with him. The more worrisome question for now was how would she get through the night without going to bed with him?

Five

She didn't want to, either, because as charming and sexy and handsome as Gabe was, he still wasn't her type. He was a wild man with a wild lifestyle like her younger brother had had, living life on the edge. And he wasn't into serious relationships, wasn't interested in commitment or marriage. She didn't want to fall in love and then have her heart broken when they said goodbye and went their separate ways.

And she certainly had no intention of getting casually involved with Gabe, either. So she needed to guard her heart—and tonight was the night to start doing her best to try.

Right now, though, wrapped in Gabe's arms, she was finding that difficult. They'd joined the others on the dance floor and hadn't missed one slow song all evening. She was resting her cheek on his shoulder when he leaned close to whisper in her ear.

"I think we've spent enough time at this shin-dig. Want to go?"

"I'm ready to go. I've done what I came to do," she said, turning. He was only inches away and she looked into the bluest eyes she had ever seen. Her heart drummed and she wanted his mouth on hers more than anything right then. But de-sire for Gabe's kisses scared her. His kisses could lead to seduction and an even bigger threat—him stealing her heart away.

Go home. Tell him good-night.

She should listen to that inner voice, thank him and then stay away from him. Instead, she was going home with him. How much willpower did she have? She couldn't even stop looking into his eyes right now.

She felt as if she had been caught in a spell and couldn't escape. How could Gabe have this kind of effect on her? It was Gabe—friend, chum, pal, buddy. Where had all this sexual appeal and steaming desire come from? Could she cope with it or did she need to call off this engagement?

She wasn't calling off the engagement. That she knew for sure. No, she'd just have to resist him. No matter what it took.

"I think tonight went well."

Gabe's comment was an understatement. In her opinion, it had gone as if she'd scripted it. Her parents had remained civil and even better was Justin's reaction.

"Thanks to you," she replied, looking at him as he drove them home, "it went even better than I had hoped. Justin certainly got the message, and so did my family. He wasn't happy, but he'll adjust and find someone who'll suit his folks just as much. My parents aren't their only friends with a daughter."

"Just because your parents are friends is no reason for the two of you to marry."

"Do I ever agree. I couldn't make any of them see that and then Justin's dad offered so many financial rewards that Justin absolutely wanted us to marry. Well, now I don't have to. You were perfect tonight. Everyone will believe us when we announce our engagement. Besides, I had a good time tonight," she said, sitting back and smiling happily at him.

"Thank you. So did I. It wasn't the stuffy, boring evening I thought it might be. Events like that at the country club I usually avoid. This one was fun, though, and I had the prettiest woman in the club for my date."

She smiled at him and patted his knee. "Thank you. We're alone and you don't have to say that."

"I mean it. You look stunning tonight. Believe me, if we weren't announcing this engagement, you would get calls, especially now that guys realize you're not locked into going out with Justin."

"I'm not interested in calls. I just want to be free and live my life my own way."

"You're on your way to your goal."

"Thanks to you."

"You can show me your gratitude when we get to my place," he said, teasing her.

She laughed. "Oh, I intend to—up to a point."

He flashed a smile at her and then focused on driving. She felt as if a mountain of worries had lifted off her shoulders. She regretted hurting her parents and Justin, but they would get over it and she couldn't spend a lifetime married to someone she didn't love. She glanced at Gabe and forgot Justin and the disagreement with her family. She'd had a wonderful evening with Gabe and his brothers and their wives. It was Gabe, though, who kept her heart racing. She was going home with him. She had told herself over and over as she spent the day getting ready for tonight that she should guard her heart and avoid falling in love with him—something she had never expected to have to worry this much about.

Gabe slowed the car and they entered a gated area and followed a tree-lined street with decorative lampposts as they wound toward his Dallas home. When it came into view, she felt surprised.

"It looks like a palace," she said, looking through a tall black wrought-iron fence at a sprawling mansion with lights shining in various windows on three floors. The well-landscaped yard held tall shade trees, leafy oaks and spreading maples. On the front lawn water glistened in a small pond with blooming lilies and in a lighted fountain with a silvery spray of water.

"Don't sound so shocked."

"I still think of you at your parents' home when we were kids."

"I haven't lived there since I left for college." Gabe drove to the back and parked beneath a carport, stepping out to go around and open her car door. "Come see my house and I'll show you your suite. If you'd like, tomorrow we can go to the ranch," he said as she stepped out to walk beside him.

He held open the door to a mudroom of sorts. The long, narrow room held rocking chairs, hat racks and coatracks on the wall, with a place for boots and shoes in a small alcove.

He took her arm. "Let's get something to drink. We can sit in the family room or go to the patio. It's a nice night."

"Sure, Gabe," she said. "But first, I want to thank you again for tonight and for what you're doing," she said, overwhelmed by having such a good friend who had come through for her and ended a huge worry in her life. She slipped her arms around him, hugged him tightly and then stood on tiptoe to kiss him.

After a startling moment that was no more than a heartbeat, his arms circled her waist and tightened, pulling her against him. His mouth pressed against hers, his tongue going deep, stroking hers as he held her close.

Her heart thudded and she tightened her arms around him. She had told herself that a few kisses out of gratitude would be acceptable and not dangerous to her heart. But now, with the first kiss, she stopped thinking about what she ought to do. Her focus was on the man holding her tightly. The man whose fingers wound in the curls of her long hair as he held her and kissed her.

And all her rules and promises to herself vanished like smoke on the wind. The only thing she wanted was to kiss him and never stop.

She ran her hand beneath Gabe's jacket to push it off. He shrugged out of it and it dropped to the floor. His elegant dress shirt was smooth to the touch, warm from his body heat. The studs in his shirt were sharp against her skin and she stepped back, reaching up to unfasten then. "These hurt," she whispered and looked up into vivid blue eyes that had darkened in passion. When she had the studs unfastened, she handed them to him. He dropped them into his pocket while she ran her hand across his chest.

"I'm not going to bed with you," she whispered, a reminder to herself as she was again caught and held by his startling blue eyes.

"Are you talking to me or to yourself?" he asked while he showered light kisses on her ear, her nape, brushing her lips with his. Her heart raced and his tantalizing light kisses fanned desire beyond anything she had ever experienced.

"I'm talking to both of us," she whispered. "Kisses of thanks for what you did tonight are the limit."

"You might have to remind me," he whispered and tightened his arms around her, settling his mouth on hers and kissing her passionately again.

Desire was a hot flame burning inside her. His touch burned away rational thought. All she could do was feel. She ran her hand beneath his unbuttoned shirt, feeling his smooth, muscled back, down to his narrow waist where she unfastened his cummerbund.

Leaning away she looked up at him and slid her arms around his neck. "You make me lose all caution and common sense."

"I hope so," he whispered and kissed away any answer she might have had.

She didn't feel his hands on her back, but was dimly aware as he pulled down the zipper to her dress.

She was crushed against him, holding him tightly while they kissed. Her heartbeat still raced. How long they kissed she didn't know. Finally, Gabe picked her up and carried her in his arms. She never once stopped kissing him to see where he was going; she didn't care. A moment later he sat down and placed her on his lap as he kissed and held her.

She felt his hands at her back, cooler air drifting over her back while he slid her zipper farther down to her waist and pushed her dress off her shoulders.

She caught the front of her dress in her fist,

holding it to cover her breasts as she leaned away slightly to look at him. His heavy-lidded gaze met hers.

"Meg, where did all this fiery sex come from?" he whispered.

"Gabe, wait. You're going too fast and in seconds our relationship will change forever."

"It already has," he said in a thick, husky voice. "We can't ever go back to a next-door-neighbor, brother-and-sister relationship, even if we promise never to touch each other again. It won't ever be the same because now we know what we do to each other and it's so fantastic, I'm still in shock."

She placed her index finger lightly on his lips. "Stop. We may not be able to go back, but we don't have to go deeper into a sexual relationship. We're not suited—"

"Darlin', we are suited—in the best way possible," he said, kissing her just above her bare shoulder. "I almost don't know which is the most stunning—kissing you or looking at you."

She pulled her dress back in place and slipped off his lap. She straightened her dress and reached back to pull up her zipper. Standing, Gabe did it for her, tugging so slowly, trailing kisses above her zipper as he moved up to lift her hair and kiss her nape. "You're gorgeous."

"Thank you," she whispered, turning around to face him and stepping back. "I'm trying to use some sense and resist you. To think a minute. I'm not into casual affairs. That kind of covers the biggest difference between us. And then, should you get serious, I could never deal with your wild lifestyle."

"Whoa, darlin'. You're talking marriage and all we've done is share a few good-night kisses." He smiled at her. "I'll show you the house and we'll have a drink and sit and talk awhile and then you can go to bed all by yourself. How's that?"

"A good idea," she said, hoping her reminder about relationships really had stopped him and made him think about the differences between them. She fought the craving she felt to walk right back into his arms, kiss him and forget common sense, caution and her worries about the future.

"Gabe, I don't want to go from one problem to another."

"I know you don't," he said, looking intently

at her, and she wondered what he really thought. "Okay, let's look at the house. So far we haven't gotten far beyond the back door.

"This back room leads into the hall with the main kitchen and an informal dining area," he said, leading the way and leaving space between them. Her gaze swept over him as he stopped in the center of the kitchen to tell her where to find things.

She didn't hear a word he said. His shirt was still open and pulled out of his trousers, the cummerbund tossed away. His chest was muscled, covered with a spread of dark curls, his stomach flat and muscled. She couldn't get her breath and she wasn't thinking straight.

She realized he had stopped talking and stood facing her, his eyes narrowed.

"I think you should show me where my room is and we should call it a night."

He closed the space between them in a few steps and wrapped his arms around her. "That's ridiculous, Meg. We can kiss and then stay friends. It's just kisses. Relax. You're blowing this all out of proportion." He took her arm lightly. "Come on, and I'll show you where your suite is, and we'll come back down here in a little while and sit and talk."

"You know, I should go to my room, close the door and not see you again tonight," she said.

He shook his head. "Nope. You wanted a fake engagement. We're getting into that and we need to do a little planning—unless you want to call all this off right now."

They stared at each other while her heart pounded. She shook her head. "No, I'm not calling anything off. We've come this far and I see freedom. Kissing you may be a problem, but it's nowhere near the problem of a lifetime with a man I don't love." She started walking down the hall. "You're right. We'll come back here and make some plans and then say good-night. You'll go your way and I'll go to my room alone. Okay?"

"Sounds like a plan. Come on. I'll show you to your suite."

He carried the bag and the carry-on she'd brought and they climbed a wide spiral staircase with a wrought-iron banister and oak steps. The staircase gave her a view of the front hall and the entryway with a huge crystal chandelier. Large contemporary paintings lined the walls along with mirrors and occasional potted palms and tropical greenery.

Upstairs, they turned for the east wing and shortly entered a room where Gabe switched on recessed lights. The room was decorated in white and taupe with charcoal accents. Contemporary steel-and-glass furniture had simple lines, and blended with the walls and white woodwork.

"This is beautiful, Gabe," she said, looking at the designs of the colored glass on the end tables.

He put her carry-on in a large walk-in closet and then set her bag on a luggage stand.

She stood in the center of the bedroom, looking at the king-size bed, the sleek chairs and sofas, glass tables and large contemporary paintings with bright strokes of red, green and blue.

More than her surroundings, she was aware of Gabe, moving around, setting up her suitcase, opening doors onto a balcony. He turned to cross the room and come back to her. "Want some time to unpack and freshen up? Or are you ready to go have a drink and make our plans?"

"It's not too early."

He placed his hands on her shoulders and toyed with locks of her hair. "No, it's not. Let's just go sit and talk about where we go from here and what we do next."

Her heart raced as she gazed into his vivid blue eyes. "I know we need to make some decisions," she whispered. Once her gaze drifted to his mouth she couldn't speak. She inhaled deeply, trying to think, to focus on her problem when all she could really do was look at him and want to put her arms around him and kiss him.

"I think first we have to decide what we'll do about...this," she was finally able to say. "I can't get this close to you without wanting to kiss you. Gabe, that wasn't something I expected and I never factored it in. You were another brother, my childhood best friend, a fun guy, someone I trust completely. But then we kissed, and suddenly it isn't that simple anymore."

He ran his hands down her sides. "No, it isn't simple. I never expected any of this hot chemistry that has exploded between us. I keep asking you if you want to call off the engagement and you keep saying no you don't."

"I don't. We've already accomplished a lot. Everyone thinks I'm dating you. That stops Justin from that very public proposal. Hooray for that one because I would never accept his proposal and I shudder to think about turning him down in front of a crowd. I still think we should go ahead and get engaged this weekend. I've told Justin we're through, but getting engaged to you will send a message not only to him, but to his parents and my family. I can get engaged to you, Gabe. I can go out with you a couple of nights this week and then say goodbye. Is that too much for you?"

"Meg, I'll be happy to take you out every day and every night this week. I can spend the week just looking at you. You're gorgeous. But when this is over, I may want you to continue to go out with me."

She shook her head. "No, you won't. And I don't want to go out with you when this is over. Gabe, we're best friends, but it ends there. I can't deal with your lifestyle and you won't want to give it up. And I can't have a casual affair and you don't want a permanent relationship. I think that covers everything between us and the answer has to be we walk away from each other and forget we ever kissed."

She looked into fathomless blue eyes that held her in their depths and made her speech empty, meaningless words. She couldn't really say anything else while her heart pounded so violently.

He brushed her hair back and framed her face with his hands as he stepped closer and gazed down at her. She couldn't move away, couldn't protest.

"You want me to forget we kissed. Meg, if I live to be a hundred, I'll remember every kiss we've shared. We have a hot chemistry between us that sets me on fire each time I'm with you." All the time he talked, his voice dropped lower, became more husky. His gaze made her heart continue to pound. Desire was intense, a pull that she tried to resist, but it became more of an ordeal to resist each time she was with him.

"Gabe, how did this happen and where did common sense go?"

"I don't know how the hell it happened, but it's

magnificent, breathtaking and too big to walk away from and ignore," he said, his voice lowering with each word as he leaned closer. She looked at his thick black hair that she wanted to tangle her fingers in. Her gaze moved to his mouth, his full, lower lip that she wanted to kiss.

A small voice continued to remind her that she did not want to fall in love. They had no future. She could really get hurt. She shouldn't kiss him.

And then there was her heart, beating with desire for him. How could she resist the most fantastic, sexiest kisses ever?

"Oh, Gabe, this is just dreadful," she whispered as he pulled her tightly against him and leaned forward to kiss her. His mouth was hard on hers, demanding, taking from her and then giving her a chance to kiss him in return.

Her world spun and she felt a dizzying plunge while at the same time, she wanted to hold him and be held by him, wanted his hard body against hers and his strong arms crushing her against him while he kissed her senseless.

Desire built as she fought the temptation to push away his shirt. Never had any other man made her respond the way Gabe did. How could this happen between them? They were buddies and had never been anything beyond buddies. Never before had there been this wild, insatiable attraction that threatened to consume her and turn her world upside down.

Pouring herself into her kiss, she clung tightly to him, aware of his strength, his arousal that pressed against her as they held each other. She let down her guard and kissed him passionately, lost in the moment and his kisses that melted all her resistance.

Gabe's hands slipped over her back, caressing her bottom and then moving to draw down the zipper to her dress and push it off her shoulders. His hands slipped to her waist and he shifted slightly as they cupped her breasts.

In seconds her bra was unfastened and pushed away and his warm hands caressed her, holding her while his thumbs lightly circled her nipples and made her gasp with pleasure as she clung to him.

"Gabe, we have to stop," she whispered, opening her eyes to look up at him. She didn't want to stop, but that small voice became more insistent, forcing her to think about her future and how she could be hurt.

While he still caressed her, he stepped back. "You're beautiful," he declared in a husky drawl. "Darlin', you're so beautiful."

She inhaled, holding his arms, closing her eyes and letting him kiss and caress her breasts for seconds before she shook her head. It was an effort to break away as she stepped back and caught his wrists. "Ah, Gabe. I can't do this. I'll fall in love with you. I never expected to want to kiss you or want you to kiss me. I didn't even think about us kissing."

She wiggled and shed her bra, pulling her dress up again. Gabe gasped for breath as much as she did.

"We should say good-night now."

He stood breathing hard while he stared at her seconds before he shook his head. "We need to talk. I'll sit out of reach and leave you alone as long as you want. Let's go get a cool drink, cookies, crackers and cheese, whatever you want.

We won't kiss again tonight unless you want to. Come on. Let's go to the kitchen."

"I'll join you in the kitchen. I'm putting on my jeans and a T-shirt and maybe you'll see me more the way you always have."

"Okay. I'll meet you in the kitchen," he said, leaning close and catching her chin between his thumb and forefinger, "but, Meg, darlin', you could come out covered from head to toe in gunnysacks and I'll never again in this lifetime see you the way I did before we kissed."

"Try," she said, narrowing her eyes at him while her heartbeat still raced and she fought walking back into his arms and going to bed with him tonight.

He smiled. "See you downstairs. I'll go step into the walk-in freezer and see if I can cool down a little. I'll try to stop thinking about you changing clothes, unless you want me to stay and help with that zipper."

"No, I don't. Aren't you getting my message?" she snapped and then realized he had been teasing as he left laughing at getting her riled up over his suggestion. She crossed the room and closed the door because she didn't want him popping back in. She let out her breath. How was she going to live in his house, go out with him, continue to kiss him and avoid falling in love with him?

Six

Gabe went downstairs and wished his body would cool down. From the moment she had opened her door to greet him for the evening, he had been in shock over her looks, on fire with wanting her in his arms and wishing he could make love to her all night long.

Why hadn't he ever noticed her like this before? Her hair made a huge difference, but he should have been able to see beyond that. Makeup made a difference, too, but again, he should have seen her natural beauty and sexy appeal. He supposed he had known her so long, he never really looked at her. He did now and he didn't want to stop looking. Blonde or brunette, headband or long, flowing hair, makeup or none, he would always see her as a beautiful woman now. She took his breath away and he ached to hold her and kiss her and seduce her.

Of all the women he knew, why did it have to be Meg who set his heart pounding? She constantly reminded him they were not well suited. That was an understatement. In too many ways, she definitely wasn't the woman for him. Not the least of which was the fact that her whole family hated him on sight, equating him with his father and never giving him a chance to prove he was different.

At the same time, in some basic, essential ways, she was the most desirable woman he had ever known, and that's what really scared him.

"Aw, hell," he whispered to himself as he walked back to his kitchen. "Dammit, Meg. Why did you come back into my life like a cyclone ripping up my world?"

His little neighbor friend, dependable, sweet Meg whom he trusted with his deepest childhood secrets and disappointments, was the woman who suddenly made him weak in the knees, dazzled him with her looks, took his breath away when he saw her and set him on fire with longing to take her to bed.

She was a gorgeous woman with silky hair and enormous, thickly lashed brown eyes, a to-die-for body that could set him aflame with desire at just a glimpse. What would she be like in bed? He had a hard-on just thinking about it. How could she do this to him with just her appearance and a few kisses? The sexiest kisses of his entire life. Oh, if he had only known in high school. It was a good thing he hadn't. He couldn't lay a hand on her back then. Her dad and older brothers would have come after him. He wouldn't have been able to live with his conscience, either.

But now she was a grown woman, over twenty-one and making her own decisions. This whole scenario of her pulling him back into her life had been because she was making her own decisions. She liked to kiss as much as he did and she couldn't resist doing it, even if she didn't like his lifestyle and knew he would never be serious no matter how much they made love or how long they lived together.

Would he have to deal with his conscience if he seduced her? He thought it over, mulling over the past hours he had spent with her, and once again, he told himself she was a grown woman, making her own decisions about her life. If she went to bed with him, it would be because she wanted to make love. She was mature enough to make her choices—otherwise she wouldn't be asking him to carry off this fake engagement.

Did she want to make love? Well, she wasn't exactly saying no to him. And she'd kissed him into a frenzy. That was not the action of a woman who didn't want to make love.

He felt better about seduction, kisses and having Meg at his house. He even felt better about the fake engagement, which had worried him at first because he didn't like the deception and hadn't thought they could convince anyone they were engaged.

Her parents already didn't like him. What would they think if they saw him as a potential in-law? As a kid, when his dad and Meg's dad had worked together, he had enjoyed spending time with her family because they were very loving. He didn't have that at home and it had been an eye-opener to be with them.

Mostly, he hadn't thought she could convince anyone they were really engaged so quickly. That had been before tonight, when the spark of that kiss had suddenly ignited into a full flame with the magic of her makeover. She had looked gorgeous, sexy and sophisticated. Put that kiss together with her lifelong honesty and he thought she probably could carry off a fake engagement.

The seduction of Meg. He remembered her stepping close, throwing her leg across his and sitting astride his lap, facing him, challenging him with a kiss that was instant heat. Just thinking about that incident made his temperature climb.

The fact that Meg would be a challenge in bed and sexy still stunned him. He wondered if he'd ever get over the shock of going from seeing her as a child to viewing her as a desirable woman. A hot, appealing, breathtaking woman. A woman he hoped and dreamed of seducing and having hours with in bed. A fantasy come to life.

Right now, when she wasn't even with him and the house was quiet, he should be relaxed after a fun evening with the best-looking woman in the county and a delicious dinner with his family. He should be mellowed out, happy.

Instead, he was on fire with wanting her, aroused, breaking into a sweat while he tried to think how he could get her into his bed.

Or was that just a fantasy? What if she didn't want seduction and he had to do the honorable thing and stay the close friend he had always been?

He felt as if he was spinning himself in circles. She had sent his life spiraling into chaos. He couldn't even think straight anymore.

He groaned and went to the bar to get a beer when he heard her approaching. His pulse raced and eagerness gripped him. It was Meg, he reminded himself. Meg, his friend who trusted him, counted on him to come through for her in all sorts of ways that a best friend would.

She walked through the door and all his good

intentions flamed into ashes as his gaze swept over her. He smiled at her and watched her cross the room toward him, remembering her with the black dress pushed to her waist, the lacy bra tossed aside and her soft, full breasts filling his hands.

She wore a bulky blue T-shirt, skintight jeans and leather moccasins. Her beautiful blond hair gave her glamour that she had never had before. The makeup she hadn't washed off just added to it, emphasizing her big, dark brown eyes. He was tempted to take her into his arms and kiss her right now.

"Wow, even dressed down you look good," he said, meaning every word. "I can't wait to take you out tomorrow night. I should have asked you out long before now."

She laughed and squeezed his hand. Locks of his dark hair fell on his forehead and she pushed them gently back off his face. "You're being ridiculous. You don't really want to take me out, but that's nice. You've had years to invite me out and you had no interest. We are not well suited and you know it."

"We're well suited enough to have a great time together. We've always had a good time together. Right now, let me get you something to drink and something to go with it. What would you like?"

"A glass of iced tea. But I'm not hungry, so I don't need anything to eat."

He stepped close. "I'd like to eat you up," he said, leaning forward to nuzzle her throat and kiss her ear. He grabbed her wrist and felt her racing pulse.

She pushed lightly against him. "Whoa, cowboy. Get my tea and pull yourself together. Remember, this is a pretend engagement and you don't have to pretend when we're alone."

"I'm not pretending," he said, gazing intently at her. "You're stunning, Meg," he said quietly. "I'm still in shock and I can't get used to the change."

"I'm still me and you've never wanted to kiss or hug or dance with me before this, so rein it in, my friend, because you and I aren't going anywhere together beyond this brief favor you're doing for me. Then it's adios and we'll probably go another year before we cross paths again. I'm not your type and you're not my type. Now, if you can comprehend all that, let's have a drink," she said, heading for his kitchen and his fridge.

He stood and watched the sway of her hips as she walked. He wanted to go after her, grab her around the waist and haul her back into his arms.

"Damn," he whispered. He needed to get her out of his hair and out of his life as soon as possible. She was right—they didn't have a future together and she wouldn't go to bed with him. She'd only keep him tied in knots in the meantime. His initial gut feeling of dread, when she first asked him for the fake engagement, had been on target. The lady was going to mess up his life for a little while and he needed to guard his heart. He had never before worried about falling in love with someone, but he worried now. He damn well didn't want to fall in love with her, but could he avoid it?

"Have a seat, Meg, and I'll get everything," he said, taking over getting drinks. She moved to the kitchen table, pulled out a chair and sat to watch him.

When he had drinks and crackers and slices of

Muenster and sharp cheddar cheese ready, he sat across from her and sipped his cold beer.

"I've been thinking, Gabe. How about getting engaged tonight?"

He swallowed hard. "That's damn quick."

"Maybe, but we've known each other all our lives. We've gone out together. It's feasible. We can plan for a wedding far in the future. This is July. How about a spring wedding, like the first week of April, and a wonderful cruise for a honeymoon? That's so far away, so no one will do anything concrete right now. In the meantime, everyone will think we're in love because I'll be living with you."

"Until April?" he asked. If he had to live in the same house with her for months, he'd have to take her to bed. Either that or he'd surely go crazy.

"No, not until April." She gave him a sassy look, as if she wasn't sure whether he was teasing her or not. "We have a deal. One month and then you're off the hook." She sipped her iced tea. "I'm sure it won't take any time for Justin to find a new girlfriend, and I'll bet he does a better job of picking one out this time. Whoever she is, she'll have his parents' approval."

"What about your folks?"

"My folks have already given up, I'm sure. My mom understands now and she'll get the family in line. I've told Justin goodbye and— Actually, he told me goodbye. He said if I went out with you, we were through. Either way, I'm free," she said, waving her arms in the air and then smiling at him.

"Suppose he's burned and wants to back off from relationships and take his time, and doesn't even date?"

"No. He'll want to show everyone that losing me means nothing. That he can pick up and go on with his life. Which I hope he does. He won't hang around waiting for me to change my mind, either. He'll be angry and he'll want to show everyone that I didn't affect his life and he can get along fine without me."

"So you want to get engaged tonight," he said, wondering again how much more upheaval she would cause in his life. "Even when it's pretend, it's a big step that gives me sweaty palms."

"That's because we're not in love. When you're in love with someone, you won't feel that way."

"Thank you, for the reassuring engagement advice," he remarked and she stuck her tongue out at him, making him grin.

He thought for a moment. "They saw us tonight at the club. Tomorrow is Sunday and we can go to my church. If we go to yours, I don't think I would be welcome. Then—"

"Of course you'd be welcome at my church. Just not with my family."

"Okay. We'll go to your church and then let's go to the ranch and come back to Dallas Tuesday. We'll try to do something special then, and let's get engaged then instead of tonight. If you're going out with me and living in my house, you won't have to date Justin."

"True. I think that's a good idea. My family will definitely not like it when they discover I'm staying with you."

"Do I need to be on guard because of your dad and grandfathers?"

As she shook her head, she laughed. "What a

thought. My grandfathers wouldn't do anything to you. My dad wouldn't, either."

"I don't agree, but we won't argue about it," he said. "If your dad does anything, it will be in the business world." And he was ready for it.

As he sat across the table from her and listened to her make plans, he had to admit only half his attention was on what she was telling him. The other half—the lower half, to be exact— was studying her. She had changed into the plain clothes he had seen her wear hundreds of times before. And they had an entire table between them, so he was nowhere near her. None of that mattered. He still wanted to pick her up and sit with her on his lap and kiss her. He didn't care what she did about the engagement or when. He just wanted her in his arms.

Despite all their differences, he knew they'd be compatible in bed. But he could never marry someone who didn't like anything he did outside of the bedroom.

Marry?

What was he thinking? It was all pretend, he

reminded himself. No one was getting married here!

He had to remember that.

He took a deep swig of his beer and tried focusing on what Meg was saying.

"Anyway, I'm so happy." She was practically wriggling with glee. "My folks won't push me to marry at all now. They certainly aren't going to want me walking down the aisle with you. Sorry." She shot him a sheepish look.

"I get it. It's okay. But if I were you, I wouldn't assume Justin is a done deal. The way you look now, he is not going to give up that easily."

As if to emphasize what he was saying, her phone buzzed. Her eyes widened in a startled look and then she pulled her phone from her pocket, looked at the caller ID and glanced in surprise at him. "It's Justin."

"Told you so." He stood up. "I'll leave you so you can talk in private. Good luck." Gabe picked up his beer and headed outside, closing the door behind him as he heard her quiet hello.

Gabe suspected Justin would put pressure

on her to marry until they announced the engagement.

That would open up another can of worms, he realized. Her family would hate him more than ever and that was a sobering fact. He was unaccustomed to anyone actively disliking him, and he had respect for her parents and grandparents, and especially liked Mason Aldridge, her rancher grandparent. He wished she didn't have to let anyone know about the engagement except Justin, but that wouldn't ever fly. It had to be all her family, too, because they were the ones really worrying her, far more than Justin was. She would have been able to deal with Justin if all the parents had stayed out of it.

He heard the door and turned as she stepped outside and joined him.

"You're right. He wants to see me and talk. He was very persistent. He said he would drop by my office next Tuesday. How do you say no to that one?"

"I guess you don't. Want me to drop by at the same time?"

She laughed. "Indeed, I don't. You two don't need to get into it. I'm sure he doesn't like you."

"Enough about Justin. Want me to surprise you with an elaborate marriage proposal? Or do you just want to keep it simple? We go out and during the evening I give you a ring and then we go tell your parents."

"Let's keep it simple because it isn't real." She thought for a moment, then said, "The grandparents that live with my parents are going to Colorado to see my aunt, so after we tell my mom and dad I'll call both sets of grandparents."

"I may have a guilty conscience every time I see Mason Aldridge."

"No, you won't. You've got nothing to feel guilty about. You're coming to my rescue with this fake engagement."

Fake engagement. The words resonated in his head. He looked at her. "Is either one of us going to have trouble remembering this engagement isn't real?"

"What you're asking is, will I want the real thing before this is over. No, my friend, I will not. All I have to do is stroll out the door on your ranch and see those big rodeo bulls you raise and sell, and know that you ride them, too. Then see your motorcycle, remember your plane, look at your sports car that will do a hundred miles an hour in the first three seconds or some other ridiculous statistic, and I promise you, I will never want the real thing from you. Not for one teeny, tiny second. And I know you won't want it from me, because you don't want the real thing anytime with any person. Right?"

"You're on target there." He saluted her with his beer bottle. "Well, we know where we stand and what we're going to do. This has turned out to be a simple deal."

She clinked his bottle with her glass. "Oh, sure, except for one little surprise—when we kiss, we both lose all rational thought and want the other person in a way that is so fierce it's scary."

"We won't even think about that part of it. Keep your distance and try to be a little remote and untouchable. I can't believe I'm saying that to you."

"I can definitely be remote and untouchable. I'll get my old hairdo back and pack my bags and move home. You'll forget all about me, especially when I'm covered in dirt."

He doubted that.

"You know, I never did ask you about your business. I'm glad it's growing and you like it. Do you get out there and mow with the guys?"

She laughed. "No. I'm a landscape designer. I plan flower beds, how yards will look—what trees will be good and where they should be planted. I hire and keep up with everything, but mostly my job is planning." She looked out at his crystal-blue pool, with a waterfall and fountain at one end. "I have an interest in a pool business in Dallas, too. They do the pools in the yards I landscape. I'm surprised you didn't let me have a shot at doing yours, but that's okay. I haven't inquired about buying a bull from you."

He smiled at her. "Maybe I'll have you come do the yard over."

She looked around. "This yard doesn't need doing over. It's beautiful, Gabe. Your pool is gorgeous and this patio—with the furniture, the big-screen television, the fire pit and the outdoor rug—it's all perfect. When we arrived, I saw your beautiful shade trees. Your oaks are marvelous. And your two magnolia trees. They're big for how long you've lived here."

"Some of the biggest ones were already on the lot. I had the house that was here razed and this one built. It's more contemporary—lots more glass and plain lines."

"You have a beautiful home."

"Thanks. Maybe we should go inside. Seems kind of warm tonight."

He held the door for her and when she walked past him, he caught a whiff of her new exotic scent and looked at the sexy sway of her hips and desire tore at him. He wanted her in his arms. What was wrong with him? Only minutes ago he all but told her he would leave her alone. Once again his libido warred with his common sense. He wanted her but he knew he shouldn't touch her. He had to avoid seducing her or he would be doing this fake engagement for real, because of a guilty conscience. And, heaven forbid, he did not want to fall in love. That hadn't ever happened and he didn't think he ran much of a risk, but Meg had a way of complicating his peaceful life. He couldn't think of many disasters as big as falling in love with Meg. She'd tear his heart into little pieces. She didn't like any part of his life—his bulls, his motorcycle, his car, his planes, nothing except him. He had to keep reminding himself of that, so he'd keep his hands off her.

"I guess I'll turn in, now that we've made our plans," she said as they walked inside. "Tomorrow we're going to your ranch after church, right?"

"Yes. I'll take the small plane."

She spun around. "No way! I'm not flying in your small plane. I'll drive to your ranch."

"But it'll take so long to drive," he protested.

She stepped toward him. "Don't worry, I'll entertain you while you drive," she said, running her hands over his chest.

He shook his head and dragged her hands away. He couldn't risk having her touch him, not when he was about to explode. "Life is full of risks. You can't live in a bubble."

"There are some risks that are unnecessary and some that are definitely bigger than others. I don't have to fly to your ranch, therefore I'm not going to fly in your small plane." She tugged her hands from him and walked away.

The sashay of her behind was the last straw. He strode forward, grabbed her and spun her around. "The hell with this, Meg." He stepped closer, not a molecule of air between them. "Here's another wild risk in life. Live a little." And he kissed her.

Seven

Meg had had every intention of going straight to bed—alone. Till now. Once Gabe's lips touched hers, every intention to resist him disappeared, along with all her warnings to herself and her sense of caution. What was the harm? A few kisses would not bind her to him. It was ridiculous to worry over a few kisses with Gabe. The minute that thought came, it was followed by big doubts. How unforgettable would Gabe be?

When his lips parted and his tongue plundered hers, she wasn't capable of any more thought. Her body overrode her mind and she wrapped her arms around him, his kiss making her feel more desired than she'd ever dreamed possible.

Her heart raced and she couldn't get her breath. She only wanted to kiss him, hold him close and run her hands over his marvelous male body.

He held her tightly, his lean, muscled body solid against her, his kiss sending her into a dizzying spiral. She thrust her hips against him. He leaned over her, kissing her and holding her while he caressed her with his other hand. His hand drifted over her nape, then down her back and beneath the shirt she wore. She had promised herself she wouldn't do this. She was putting her future, her heart at risk. She was taking the peace that she had finally achieved, turning right around and risking it all for Gabe's kisses. He could break her heart. If she made love with him, she would be in love with him, and that would lead to the worst kind of heartbreak because she had known him all her life and he was important in her life. Every second she touched and kissed him, she was wading deeper into a dangerous pool of heartbreak. She had never been emotionally invested in Justin. She was in Gabe. And that put her in danger.

Yet how badly she wanted his arms around her and his mouth on hers. Just a little longer, she told herself. How bad could it be? How could she lose her heart over kisses? Over just one night of love? Or was she simply fooling herself in order to shut out the sensible warnings of disaster?

Right now she couldn't answer that, not when her heart hammered with excitement, when desire burned hot through her fingertips that ran over his chest.

"You're a beautiful woman, darlin'. You can't imagine what you do to me," he whispered.

He kissed her again, stroking her sensuously with his tongue as he toyed with her breasts, his breath warm, his attention exciting. She ran her hands over his strong shoulders, wanting to pull him even closer, wanting him inside her.

She pulled back to drag in air. "You're pure temptation," she whispered. "You're taking me where I vowed I wouldn't go."

"I'll stop when you tell me to," he rasped out, his hands and tongue roaming over her. "Ah, you are so beautiful, so hot."

He tangled his fingers in her hair, tilting her

face up so he could look into her eyes. She felt caught and held again by his blue eyes that mesmerized her and flashed so much blatant desire she couldn't get her breath.

Wrapping his arms around her, he pulled her tightly against him. He was on fire, his manhood thick and hard and ready to love.

This would be a commitment for her while it would be no such thing for Gabe. Was that what she wanted? If they made love tonight, she would feel a bond with him that he would never feel. Could she live with that? Was she moving closer to a big heartache? She was torn between wanting him and being sensible and keeping her distance.

She ran her fingers over his nape, aching to have him inside her, wishing to be one with him, desiring all of him. She wanted his loving all through the night and she knew he would give her that if she let him. But that tiny voice of caution would not remain silent. It kept calling out to her, begging her to be wary.

Gabe would never want anything long-term and she wouldn't want it even if he did. She couldn't deal with his wild ways, so why was she getting herself more entangled with him by the minute?

"Gabe, wait," she said, leaning away from him. "This is too fast and too far for me. I just can't take making love the casual way you do."

She placed her hand on his chest as she shook her head. "Besides that, suppose we have sex and it's the most fantastic sex ever, like our kissing is fantastic. Suppose sex between us is that way. How are you going to live with that?"

Gabe blew out a hot breath and she felt his arms loosen their hold on her. "Darlin', you sure know how to kill the moment. Holy hell."

"I have definitely and obviously not killed the moment for you," she said, glancing down at the hardness in his slacks. "We're going to be together for a while. I'm going to live at your house, maybe for the rest of the month. We have time. There is no need to jump into bed tonight. Let's stop and think. Suppose sex is the most spectacular thing ever between us—"

He groaned and placed his hands on his hips. "You can stop. We'll quit for now. C'mon. I'll see you upstairs and tomorrow will be another day, as someone famous said."

She frowned, staring at him. "You think about us, Gabe."

"As if I could think about anything else."

She faced him, taking him in. His hair, a tangle of dark waves, fell on his forehead. His broad shoulders made her draw a deep breath as her gaze ran across his well-muscled chest.

"Meg, my life was quiet and peaceful and uneventful until you came back into it. I'll tell you, in all my experience with women, you're unique."

"I find that a compliment."

"Take it how you will. You were a fun special friend when we were kids, but I never thought of you as unique. Tonight's a first in my life. I've never been asked to stop for the reason you gave me. The hell of it is—you make a degree of sense. Are you even listening to me?"

"Of course I am," she said, looking up at him.

"Sleep is shot to hell for the next few hours. I'm going to have an icy shower and come back here and drink a beer. If you want to join me, you're welcome to."

"I doubt if I'll sleep, either. I'll join you here in a little while," she said. She took one last long look, her gaze running to his toes and back up to find him watching her.

"You're incredibly sexy," she whispered. "I'm going while I still can."

"Thank you, I think, for the 'incredibly sexy' remark, although that parting shot isn't doing anything to cool me down."

"I'm gone," she called over her shoulder, hurrying out of the room before she walked back into his arms and into his bed for the night.

Gabe watched her go. Her fabulous blond hair swung with each step and it took an effort to keep from going after her.

He recalled all those initial feelings, days ago, when he had watched her come up his drive and then into his house and into his life again. Those feelings that said trouble was coming had been right. He had never known another woman like her, never been sexually involved with one. Right now, as much trouble as she was, he still wanted her. If she turned around and came right back and walked into his arms, he would take her to bed with him for the night, and for the week if she would let him. And then she would worry the hell out of him, even if she didn't say anything about what they were doing. Except she would say plenty.

She had him tied in knots and he hadn't even slept with her. And she was causing him sizable grief. In addition, her dad had threatened him, which was probably an empty threat, but her family definitely disliked him. After his dad and Meg's had split, Gabe learned later, when he was grown, his dad had pulled some sneaky dealings to buy out her father for way less than he should have been worth as a partner. Her father had tried to retaliate and hurt Dirkson's business, trying to outbid him on land deals and drilling rights, but it was like a fly buzzing around a bull. Dirkson Callahan hadn't been hurt, and it had left the Aldridges bitter and angry ever since.

Mason Aldridge, her rancher grandfather, was the least angry and did speak to Gabe, probably because they knew each other through cattle sales and rodeos and ranch activities. Gabe respected her grandfather and Mason seemed respectful of Gabe. Whatever happened, Gabe just didn't want to get into a business struggle or any other feud with her family, at least no more than they already had.

Her father had warned him, and Gabe had no intention of hurting Meg, but she was the earnest type who counted on certain things and would get hurt if she didn't get them. If he slept with her, would she expect him to marry her? She had to realize, given his reputation, that he certainly had no intention of walking down the aisle after taking her to bed. She should know that, since she had talked about it often.

Gabe gathered his things and went to his room. As he stripped off his clothes, his thoughts kept going back to the past hour with Meg. It was a crime how sexy she had turned out to be. He was on fire just thinking about her and he wanted her more than ever. He had a feeling a cold shower wouldn't do the trick tonight. It would take a soak in an icy lake to cool his body down.

Why, oh, why, did his little childhood chum set him ablaze just by entering the room? As absurd as it was, the sight of her had jolted him, because he had never for one split second expected her to arouse him so instantly.

And that silly argument of hers that sex between them might be too great? It had almost made him laugh, except the prospect had made him hard from wanting her. If it turned out to be the most fantastic sex ever, he would find that a welcome problem.

He scoffed to himself as he turned on the shower. All the way to cold.

The little girl next door...

Only she wasn't the little girl next door now. She was a stunning blonde who could blow him away. And she came with all kinds of trouble— her fear of planes, fast cars, rodeo riders, all the things he thought were great, fun or just downright convenient. She had a family who hated him. She wanted commitment and marriage if she shared her bed. It was a litany that was becoming far too familiar, but he had to keep reminding himself why he should view the lady as off-limits. Big-time off-limits. Meg would be nothing but trouble in his life if he seduced her.

She already was a bushel of trouble. Why didn't that prospect cool him down?

Gabe groaned as he stepped into the shower, gritting his teeth at the cold and hoping it would freeze his libido. If only there were some spigot he could turn on to stop thinking about her and remembering how she looked and kissed—that's what he desperately needed.

He tried to think of something else to get her out of his thoughts. Another woman wouldn't do it. Business deals wouldn't, either. Meg trumped them all. Little Meg, who had him in knots and shivering in an icy shower, still unable to stop thinking about kissing her.

He had to get a grip because his thoughts were taking him to dangerous places. He started to think that it might not be the worst thing in his life if they made love and his conscience forced him into proposing to her. He expected to shudder at the thought, but not even that prospect stopped him from wanting her. And that scared him.

After a long shower, he pulled on a short-sleeved navy Western shirt and jeans. He took his time, but finally went downstairs and found her outside on his patio. He got a cold beer and joined her.

"Hi. Is it cool enough out here now?" he asked, his gaze drifting over her. She wore another loose-fitting black T-shirt and cutoffs that left her legs bare. It didn't matter what she wore, she looked great and he could remember exactly how she had looked naked from the waist up.

"It's cool enough, and it's so quiet out here. All I hear is the splashing water from the fountain, which is such a relaxing sound." She laid her head back against the seat back and stretched her long legs in front of her.

He couldn't help but think how perfect she looked sitting in his backyard. As if she belonged here.

"I'll miss you when this is over."

She turned to him, her face visible in the dim patio light. "No, you won't. We haven't hung out together for quite a few years. Not like we used to. After this is over, we'll go our separate ways again." She gave him a grin. "I'll read about you in Texas magazines or in the society pages."

He put his hands up. "Not me. I won't be in many society pages. My mom maybe, when she's here, which is seldom. My dad even less, and he keeps a low profile since he's gotten older."

"You expect me to believe you're a hermit? I know you too well, Gabe Callahan."

"Oh, I get around," he retorted, "but I tend to do my trolling out of the public eye." He shrugged. "Never had any complaints from the women I've dated."

She laughed and her whole face seemed to light up. "And I'm guessing that's a fair number of women, from what I've heard."

Gabe was not the type to kiss and tell. He simply shrugged and took a draft of beer.

She turned to him then, and sat up, suddenly serious. "Don't you ever want to get married, Gabe?"

"Sure, someday, but I'm young and I'm not ready now. I don't want to be tied down and I haven't found the right woman, anyway."

"I seriously doubt if she exists," she said and he grinned.

"Sure she does. I just don't know her yet. I

could ask you the same question. Don't you ever want to get married?"

"Of course I do, but I want the right man and Justin definitely isn't him." She picked up her beer bottle. "But I think Justin has started to become history in my life, thanks to you. You're a real buddy and you came through for me in the best possible way."

"I can do even better if you'd let me," he said, his voice becoming husky.

"You have a one-track mind."

"If I do, it's because you're a good-looking, appealing woman who is fantastic to kiss." He stood up and picked her up, sitting back in his chair with her on his lap. "Maybe I do have a one-track mind where you're concerned," he said, running one hand lightly up her bare leg, his fingers slipping beneath her shorts slightly to caress her. He had limited access, but her soft, smooth inner thighs made him want to peel away the cutoffs. "I don't know how you expect me to think about other things when you dress like this. You're beautiful, Meg. You know what you do to me when we kiss. I can't stop wanting you or forget about that."

As he talked, he caressed her nape with his other hand, kissed her ear, brushed her lips with his and then paused to look at her. There was enough light that he could see her eyes were heavy lidded, her focus on his mouth. He leaned close to kiss her, pulling her tightly against him.

She wound her arms around his neck and kissed him in return, and he wanted her more than he had earlier. He picked her up and moved to a chaise longue and stretched out with her beside him, holding her close the whole time while he kissed her.

Lying beside her was an irresistible temptation. He tried to take time, to not push her, although at the moment she seemed as eager as he was. He ran his hand beneath her shirt, then shifted her slightly to unfasten the front catch to her lacy bra and pushed it away, pulling her shirt high to allow him to hold and caress her breasts.

She gasped with pleasure. "We weren't going to do this tonight," she whispered as she showered kisses on his jaw, his throat, his shoulder, unbuttoning his shirt and running her hand over his chest. In minutes she leaned away to look at him. "I need to catch my breath."

He nodded. He stood and took her hand. "Come on. We'll go inside."

"Inside and upstairs to our own suites," she added. "That's the safest plan. Tomorrow it's church and then the drive to your ranch."

"Whatever the lady wants," he said.

It wasn't what he wanted. Not by a long shot.

At the door to her suite, Meg turned and slipped her arms around his neck, leaning close to kiss him. Then she stepped back and opened her door. "This has been a wonderful evening, Gabe. Thank you."

He shook his head at her. "Darlin', you are a bundle of mixed signals. One minute you want to kiss me and the next minute you don't."

"Not so mixed. I want to kiss, but common sense takes over now and then."

He took a deep breath. "I don't recall you being this much trouble when we were kids."

"We had a simpler life when we were kids.

You're a year older and could usually get your way or beat me in games so you didn't view me as trouble. I still don't see you as trouble." She glanced down at his hands, which were reaching out to pull her close. She grinned and said, "Well, maybe some trouble." She partially closed the door, needing that physical barrier between them.

"Still, Gabe, I'm so grateful to you for getting me out of the situation with my family and Justin. Remember," she said, "I'll do some big favor for you someday if you need me to help with a problem."

She smiled as she entered her suite, closing the door and letting out her breath. "If you only knew how much trouble you really are," she whispered.

She wanted to be in his arms, wanted his loving, wanted to be in his bed right now.

She decided to take her own advice and at least take tonight to think about her future and what she wanted to do. If she slept with Gabe—and supposing the sex was super—would she be able to walk away with her heart intact? Or would it be broken?

There would be no long-term relationship, no

future with Gabe, so she needed to come to a firm decision. Did she want to miss this chance to make love with him?

She wondered if she could sleep at all. Could Gabe sleep or was he going to lie awake and think about making love?

Sunday after church they got into Gabe's black sports car. He knew he would have to stay at the speed limit or lower or his passenger would be unhappy and let him know it.

She had come downstairs this morning, dressed in a tailored summer suit of pale-blue-and-white-striped cotton with a pale blue blouse and high-heeled blue sandals. Her hair was still in spiral curls and fell freely on both sides of her face, so she hadn't reverted to her old hairstyle. And even in the tailored clothes that covered her, she took his breath away.

They went to church together and sat far from her family, but she left Gabe to talk to them after the service was over. As he headed toward his car, he stopped to talk to friends while the church crowd thinned. Each time he glanced at Meg, she was talking to her mother, and both of them looked engrossed in their conversation.

He hoped she was getting across to her mother her feelings about Justin and he might escape this month-long fake engagement, but he suspected that was highly unlikely.

"Gabe, wait up," a man called, and he turned to see his friend Marc Medina so he stopped and smiled.

"Megan, I see you're with Gabe Callahan this morning," her mother said as Meg walked up. Her father was talking to a friend and farther away from them.

"Yes, I am. We went out together last night and today he's taking me to see his ranch. Where are Lolo and Grandpa Harry?"

"They left for Colorado already. So Justin really is out of your life."

"Yes, he is. He never really was in my life as far as I was concerned."

Her mother frowned. "Megan, please think about what you're doing by going with Gabe Callahan. You know how the family feels about the Callahans."

"Mom, that is your generation. My generation has no problem with the younger Callahans. Gabe and I have been friends forever, as you know, and it's fun to be with him."

Her mother frowned as she stared at Meg. "I hope we didn't push you into doing something foolish."

"I assume you mean pushing me into going out with Gabe. We've been friends almost since we were toddlers. I like being with him," she said, glancing around to see Gabe standing in the shade of a tree, talking to a friend.

"Gabe is waiting. I'll talk to you later."

"Take care. I love you."

She hugged her mother. "I love you, too." She looked at her mother. "I know you mean well and want me to be happy."

"That's what's important."

"I better run," she said, turning to hurry across the lot to Gabe. He stood alone in the shade now, his arms folded as he waited. Her heart beat faster when she looked at him. He was dressed for church in a charcoal Western-style suit, his black boots and black Stetson. They had already planned to drive back to his house to change clothes and get some of her things before leaving for his ranch.

"Thank you for waiting so patiently," she said. "Wait until we're at your house. I'm going to give you a giant hug and jump up and down for joy. My mom finally gets it that I do not want to date Justin, much less marry him."

Gabe laughed. "Whoa, slow down. I got what you said, but you sound like Horace Grayson when he's auctioning cattle."

Feeling giddy, she laughed. "I'm just so happy. She finally understands."

Gabe held the car door open and she stepped forward to get in, but paused in front of him, with only inches between them.

"You handsome devil. You are the greatest friend ever and if we weren't on the church grounds, I'd hug you right now. You did it. See? Taking me out started opening the doors to my freedom. Hooray!"

She saw him glance around and then he ushered her into the car. "Get in before someone else comes over to talk and we never get out of here."

Smiling at him, she slid into the seat and he closed the door. She watched him walk around the car, something she enjoyed doing because he was so handsome in his Sunday outfit. He would be handsome out of his Sunday outfit, too, she was sure.

He sat behind the wheel, buckled his seat belt and started the car, driving slowly out of the lot.

Meg turned toward him as much as she could with a seat belt on. "I'm so happy, I can't sit still. I'm free. I owe it all to you. What a friend you are."

"You just keep those thoughts in your pretty head until we get to my house."

"I couldn't get rid of these thoughts right now if I tried. I feel as if I could fly out of this car."

"While you're on this high, is there any chance you'd like a real thrill and would let me fly you to the ranch?"

"Whoa, you know how to kill the moment, too, Gabe," she said. "No, I haven't changed my mind about flying in one of those little planes. I don't care how fancy or expensive it is. I don't like to fly in the big ones either, for that matter. I don't go anywhere so it isn't an issue. I'll drive to the ranch with or without you."

"I'll take you," he said, patting her leg. "I just gave it a shot. You're so exuberant, I thought I might get you in a plane."

"Sorry, not today." As euphoric as she was, noth-ing would get her in a plane.

"Want to get brunch now at someplace nice, or would you rather change, head for the ranch and eat a burger on the way?" Gabe asked as he drove. "Personally, I vote for the Sunday brunch at my favorite restaurant."

"I agree," she said. "And I'll try to control my gratitude and my excitement."

"You can bottle up all that gratitude and excite-ment while we eat and then uncork it when we're in the privacy of my house."

It was two hours later when they left the res-taurant and he drove them to his Dallas home in a gated community.

Turning to go through the big gate that opened

automatically for his car, he entered the subdivision. In minutes he went through another gate that surrounded his place. Finally, he slowed and stopped at the back of his house and went around to open her door. Before he could, she hopped out and kissed his cheek.

"Thanks a million, my friend. Don't forget my offer. I'm ready, willing and able to do something for you."

She instantly regretted her words when she saw the flare of desire in his blue eyes. She felt heat climb into her cheeks at her unwitting innuendo. Which was so unlike her. She'd never been embarrassed in front of Gabe.

"Besides going to bed, I mean," she clarified, smiling at him.

He laughed. "Meg, in some ways you haven't changed at all. At the same time, you have changed in the most delightful fashion possible. Darlin', I'm glad to be of help to you. Even though you've made a wreck out of me, I wouldn't have missed this week for the world."

"I'm so happy, I can't be still."

He reached out to draw her into his embrace,

leaning close to kiss her, a possessive, demanding kiss that made her forget her resolution to avoid kisses and sex. Gabe held her close, kissing her into scalding desire.

She wanted more, so much more.

Did she want to keep saying no and maybe miss the most dazzling sex ever?

What they did to each other was amazing—she wanted to pursue that and make love with him because it had to be fabulous. But if it was that awesome, could she keep from giving him her heart, her love, along with her body? Could she make love with him and then just walk away, heart intact, the way he would?

That was the big question she faced and she didn't have an answer.

"Gabe, I'm still thinking about this," she whispered. "I can't resist kissing you but I'm not ready to go to bed with you. That's just the way I am. It'll be complicated if I make love with you."

"Will it ever, darlin'," he said, his gaze roaming over her.

"Let's go change. I'll get the rest of my things

I want to take and we can leave for the ranch," she said.

Together they went upstairs and then parted, each to their suites.

She entered hers, closed the door and saw the vivid reflection of her eyes in the mirror. Could Gabe see what she detected so clearly there? Desire.

It was no secret that she wanted him. Whether she should act on it was the real issue.

If she refused to sleep with him and they parted, would she always feel she had missed something special? Would she regret not making love with him?

Someday she hoped she would fall in love and marry a man who was similar to her, who wanted what she wanted. Someone who led a regular life and didn't raise bulls and ride them, fly his own small plane, do all the wild things Gabe did. But for now…was she about to pass up something special that she would always remember?

Would she fall in love if she went to bed with him tonight at his ranch? She had to be able to answer no to that question or else say no to him.

She'd have to lock her heart away and enjoy a physical time with him and then leave him the way he would leave her. No strings, no ties, no commitment, no love. Could she do that, especially when it was with her best friend and the sexiest man she knew? Or would she open herself up for heartbreak?

Eight

It was late afternoon when his ranch house came into view. She looked at the long, one-story stacked-stone house with rustic wood columns along the wraparound porch and a large porte cochere to the east of the building. She admired the landscaped, fenced-in front yard with berms of mature oak trees.

"You have a beautiful place," she said. "Great landscaping with your berms."

"I'm glad you like it." He parked in the shade beneath the porte cochere and walked around to hold the car door open for her. Desire kept her acutely aware of him and her gaze raked over his broad shoulders covered with a navy cotton shirt that was tucked into jeans and one of his wide, hand-tooled leather belts, complete with a big silver belt buckle she assumed he had won riding a bull or accomplishing some other rodeo achievement. Ironically, they had both changed into jeans and navy shirts, and they had laughed about dressing alike.

"Come in and let me show you around," he said when she stepped out of his car. He picked up her bag and retrieved her carry-on and as they walked in, she was aware of him beside her.

She entered into the kitchen, well equipped with state-of-the-art appliances and a tan-and-white decor. As they walked farther into the house, she glanced at rooms off the wide main hall, and finally he showed her to the suite where she would stay. It had a separate sitting room with a wall of glass and sliding glass doors that opened onto the back porch. A few steps led down to a wide patio with an outdoor carpet, cushioned chairs and sofas, tables, a fire pit, a large television and an outdoor kitchen. Beyond it was a curving swimming pool with a waterfall and two slides.

"This is beautiful, Gabe," she said as she looked outside. "You have everything the way you like it."

But when she turned around, the picturesque sight of his backyard paled in comparison to Gabe. He was hefting her bags onto a luggage stand, his shirt pulled across his broad shoulders and his biceps flexed. Memories of their kisses before they left Dallas were still vivid in her mind, and she felt desire once again flooding her.

"Do you—" He set down her bags and glanced at her, and whatever he was about to ask her died on his lips.

She no longer had to wonder, as she had back in Dallas hours ago, whether he could see the desire in her eyes. Clearly he did.

His gaze locked with hers as he strode across to her. He wrapped his arms around her and tilted her chin up. She looked into his eyes, the blue darkened by passion—eyes that mirrored the desire she felt.

"Ah, darlin'," he said as he leaned down to kiss her.

Letting go of her usual caution, doubts and worries, she clung to him as eagerness filled her. Making her decision, she expected she could live with it and hoped she had made the right choice.

His scalding kiss was possessive and passionate, making her feel as if she belonged in his arms. She experienced a bond of friendship with him that she didn't have with any other man she had ever known. Because of that and his kisses that set her ablaze with an incredibly intense longing, she wanted his loving, his hands and mouth on her, his body available for her to touch and kiss. Most of all, she wanted to pleasure him, to caress and kiss him. She longed to pour out some of what she felt for him, trying to convey how happy she was to have him in her life again, even if it would be brief.

"You're so good to me," she whispered, thinking he truly was her best friend and had stuck by her when she needed him, both as a child and now as an adult. Their kisses were stupendous. Were they so great because it was Gabe? Because friendship made it more intense? Or was it some other chemistry they conjured up when they were together? She didn't know. At the moment she only knew she wanted him, needed to draw him closer, keep him close. She longed to love him and his awesome male body that made her tremble with desire.

She was about to make a commitment when she knew there would be no commitment from him. But he would always be honest and up front with her. She had already decided to live with that and, hopefully, to walk away without leaving behind her heart. This time in his arms, in his bed, couldn't change her life unless she let it. She knew his feelings and understood them. They were close, and this intimacy would be one more link in their chain of timeless friendship.

She stopped thinking about it. She was with Gabe and she wanted to make love with him.

Holding her, he leaned back slightly to look at her, a piercing look filled with unspoken questions. "You know what you want. This is a turnaround."

"Not really. We're friends. The closest of friends,

which changes everything and makes intimacy something special. I can guard my heart as you will yours, and at the same time, that friendship will shine through and become special."

He drew her close to kiss her again, a slow, tantalizing kiss as his tongue thrust deep, stroked hers, touched the corners of her mouth and moved so lightly over her lower lip. All teasing strokes that built a physical need to kiss even more passionately.

She drew his head down and stood on tiptoe to kiss him, tangling her tongue with his, wanting to bind him to her for the next hour, to be as close as they could.

He raised his head slightly. His breath was ragged and his gaze was piercing. "You are unpredictable, unforgettable, special. I want this. Oh, baby, do I want this, but intimacy will change our friendship forever."

"I know."

His gaze faltered a mere second. "I'm not into commitment, Meg. Don't think you'll change me."

She smiled at him. "I'm not planning on changing you. I know I couldn't possibly. And you're not going to change me. See, you're being a friend right now. You know I don't casually make love and you're giving me a chance to stop and think twice. But, Gabe, I know what I'm doing."

He stared at her as if weighing what she'd said and trying to come to a conclusion about how it would affect him. "I've never known a woman like you. I want you, darlin', even though you complicate the hell out of life." And with that he leaned down to kiss her and end their discussion.

While longing rocked her, she ran her hands over him. Her fingers worked swiftly to unbutton his shirt and push it away. As soon as she did, she tangled her fingers in a smattering of crisp chest curls while her other hand ran over his muscled shoulders. He was strong, fit, in peak condition, and his body was the perfect male specimen. She couldn't wait one more moment for the intimacy, the closeness that she'd resisted.

With a trembling hand she unbuckled his belt and pulled it free to drop it with a clatter. As she did, he pulled her shirt over her head, unclasped her bra and tossed them aside. His jeans went next, and he paused to yank them off, along with his boots and socks. Placing his hands lightly on her hips, he held her away to look at her. His gaze was a slow perusal that made her tingle as if his fingers caressed her. Swiftly, he unfastened her jeans and pushed them down, along with her panties. As she stepped out of them, he cupped her breasts in his warm hands, stroking their rosy tips with his thumbs and making her gasp with pleasure.

"You're beautiful, so beautiful," he whispered. "You don't know what you do to me."

Closing her eyes momentarily, she clung to his forearms as he caressed her and streaks of pleasure stirred her, making her want him more than ever. It seemed right, to be with him and kiss and caress him.

She pulled away his briefs to free his thick, hard shaft. She drew a deep breath as she looked at his body, a body that thrilled her and made her ache to touch him.

He picked her up and carried her into her bedroom to place her on the bed. He lay beside her, drawing her into his embrace, tangling his legs with hers while he kissed her—a deep, insistent kiss.

Stroking her hair away from her face, he paused to gaze intently at her. "You can't ever know how badly I've wanted to make love to you. You're a beautiful woman. You'll never know how much you excite me."

She kissed him and his fingers tangled in her hair while his arm held her against him. He was hard and she wanted to touch and explore his body. Right now, his kisses were sending her pulse racing and making her want him more than ever. He was important to her, part of her life, and now they would be closer than ever, sharing intimate moments that she hadn't expected to ever have happen. She had made love only a few times in her life, but never with anyone like him. She trembled with need and with wanting, more than she would have ever dreamed possible. She intended to seize the moment and make a memory that she would always have.

Shifting, he moved to caress her ankles, stroking, trailing his tongue slowly over her, kissing her as he moved up between her legs, running his tongue lightly on her inner thigh, making her writhe and want him more than ever. Her hands lightly drifted over his muscled thighs, higher over his hard butt and his narrow waist. His strong body was a marvel to her and she hoped to excite him as much as he excited her.

Arching her hips against him, she did what she could to give him more access, wanting to be touched more deeply.

Trailing kisses along her thigh, he moved higher while his fingers caressed her between her legs, stroking her, creating tension that built as she arched her back and thrust her hips against his hand.

Shifting her legs over his shoulders, he had access to her and ran his tongue over her. She gasped and cried out with pleasure, straining against him. "Gabe, please," she cried. All her focus was on wanting him inside her.

They shifted and she sat up, getting on her knees. When she looked into his eyes, her heart pounded. Eagerly, she wrapped her arms around him and kissed him passionately, pouring out her hunger for all of him. She trailed her hands over him and then leaned away to pull him down on the bed.

Trying to excite him as he had her, she lightly stroked him while running her tongue along his throat, across his chest, down over his belly and then along his thick rod. Holding his hard shaft, she kissed him while her other hand drifted between his legs, stroking him, toying so lightly with him and making him writhe beneath her touch. He gasped and tangled his fingers in her hair while letting her continue to pleasure him.

With another groan, he sat up to kiss her passionately, his hands cupping her breasts. He shifted, kissing her ear and whispering, "You don't know what you do to me. You're gorgeous, so incredibly sexy."

He leaned down to kiss first one breast and then the other, running his tongue over the taut peaks. One hand held her breast as the other hand went between her legs to stroke her.

She moaned with pleasure, trying to caress him in return. He paused to step off the bed and retrieve his jeans. Digging out a billfold, he returned to put on a condom.

Watching him, her heart raced. Exuding energy, he was every inch a strong, handsome, exciting man. She parted her legs, arching her back, eager for him as he came down to kiss her and press her back to the bed.

He entered her slowly, in control while he thrust in her and then almost withdrew. She gasped and cried out, pulling him closer as electrifying pleasure streaked through her. He filled her, still going slowly, building her excitement and desire. She gasped, wanting him, trying to pull his hips closer as he withdrew slightly again and was still, need making her desperate for him. She wrapped her long legs around him and pulled him closer while he again thrust slowly into her.

"Gabe, I want you inside me, all of you," she whispered, running her hands over him and raising her hips to meet him.

He thrust deeper, withdrawing slowly and then moving faster while she cried out and clung to him. In seconds he pumped faster, building her need.

She clung tightly to him, her legs locked around him as finally he let go of his control and pumped hard and fast. Her world was sensation and need that tore at her until she cried out with pleasure.

Release burst in a climax, her pounding heart shutting out other sounds as they still rocked wildly together, and then he shuddered with his own climax, taking her to another one. Pleasure spilled over her and she dug her hands into his buttocks as she moved with him.

Hot and damp, she gradually slowed while still gasping for breath. She held him tightly in her arms, her legs still clasped around him, both of them still united, and for this moment they were one.

Joy filled her as much as physical satisfaction. She embraced him tightly, still tingling and satiated. For this moment in time, she didn't want to let him go. Holding him pressed against her heart with their bodies joined, she wanted to keep him close for a while longer and not have to think beyond the moment.

Her breathing and her pounding heart were beginning to return to normal. Gabe turned his head to shower light kisses on her face and throat. While he did, she ran her fingers down his smooth back and over his buttocks, down on his muscled thighs, feeling the short curly hairs on his thighs against her palms.

Her hands came up again, traveling over him, and she tangled her fingers in his hair at the back of his head.

He rose up slightly to look into her eyes. "You were right. We're awesome together," he said solemnly. His usual joking and humor had disappeared as he looked at her intently.

"I keep catching you looking at me as if you have never seen me before in your life," she said softly.

"I wonder if I have. Your kisses blow me away. Making love is the best. I'm reeling in shock again. You did it with your first kiss. You stunned me again with your makeover. This is the third big surprise."

Smiling, she ran her fingers lightly along his jaw, feeling the short stubble. "It was fantastic. I don't quite have the experience you do to make comparisons, but sometimes you know something's special without having to compare it to anything else."

He turned on his side, holding her close so they faced each other. Their legs were entwined, their arms wrapped around each other.

She reached up to comb unruly locks of black hair off his forehead with her fingers. "It's crazy to think I just had the best sex of my life with my best friend in the whole wide world. I think my best friend should be female, but we won't tell anyone." She laughed and he did, too. "I know I'll always be able to count on you. You can count on me. If you need me, you let me know."

"I may need you again tonight," he said, grinding himself against her.

She smiled. "That wasn't what I was referring to."

"You know, I suspect when the dust settles, I'm going to discover that you've complicated my life beyond belief."

She shook her head. "I will do no such thing. Soon you'll say goodbye and you'll call and keep in touch."

"That might not happen quite as soon as you think."

"It'll happen when we can call off our fake engagement—which I think may be sooner than the end of the month. My mom got it. I'm sure Justin will be so furious that he'll stop pursuing me in spite of all his dad's offers. With that stupid old feud between our families, my parents will certainly be happy that I didn't marry you. They don't know how adorable you are." She tweaked his nose. "Back when we were little and you were at our house a lot, my mother and grandmother thought you were adorable, so I don't think they really dislike you as much as they dislike your dad."

"Frankly, I hope you're right. I really don't like to get blamed for things he's done."

Gabe pulled her close to hold her and she nestled against him.

"Tonight, I want you to stay right here with me," he said.

"It's where I want to be also," she said, smiling. "I'll stay tonight."

"I'm thinking," he mused aloud. "Maybe we shouldn't go back to Dallas until Wednesday."

"We should stick to our original plan. We go back Tuesday and announce our engagement.

I'll be staying at your house so it won't matter whether we're on the ranch or in Dallas, unless you have something pressing here."

"No, I don't. I just don't have as many interruptions here and I really don't want interruptions—or to share you with anyone."

"That's nice," she said, drawing her fingers over his shoulder and bicep, down along his arm. "You'll have to share me because I have a business to run," she pointed out. "We need to go out Tuesday night and that's when we'll get engaged and tell everyone. But when we go back to Dallas, I'll be staying at your house."

"So far, that's the best part of this plan," he said, winding long locks of blond curls around his fingers and letting them fall to pick them up again. His fingers lightly brushed her ear, every contact making her tingle.

"Later in the week or over the weekend, take a day so we can come back to the ranch. I want you to myself. You can get a day off because you own the business. Better still, take a couple of days off so we can be uninterrupted." He nuzzled her neck while he ran his fingers across her narrow waist then drifted lower, until she caught his hand and placed it at her waist again.

"Let me catch my breath," she said. She nestled against him, loving the feel of his arms around her, enjoying being with him, talking, touching and kissing each other. It was an idyll that would end when the fake engagement ended.

"This will be a big week in my life," she said. "It already is a big week because I'm here in bed with you. I think by the end of the week I'll be ready to take a day or two off. That's probably a good idea in a lot of ways."

"I think it's a fantastic idea, darlin'. A day we both need."

She smiled. "You don't *need* any such thing," she said. "It's a day we both want."

"Oh, I need you, Meg. You're special in my life," he said, his words warming her all over.

"How I wish that were true, Gabe, but I know better."

After a moment, during which time she continued stroking his back and winding her fingers in his hair, she said, "I've been thinking. I'm sorry that this is going to hurt my family, but they've pushed me into a corner trying to get me to marry someone I don't love."

"By this time next year you won't give any of that much thought, so don't worry too much about it now." He looked into her eyes, making her heart skip a beat, before he leaned closer to kiss her.

She wound her arms around his neck and kissed him back, their tongues stroking, hot and wet, each touch making her want to make love again. She held him tightly, enjoying being happy in his arms and refusing to think about the future. In minutes he rolled on his back and lifted her on top of him. She kissed him, sitting astride him.

As he fondled her breasts, making her need him again, she felt him harden beneath her. In minutes, each knowing when the other was ready, she rose up, then eased down on him. As he entered her, she closed her eyes and threw her head back, riding him as he bucked beneath her.

He thrust slowly, making her moan with pleasure as he fondled her breasts. She pumped with him, moving faster, tension and need building with her until she could not contain it.

When she climaxed, she cried out. Thrusting faster, he reached his climax. Then, finally, she fell on top of him. She held him and turned her head to kiss him, feathery kisses along his shoulder, his neck and his jaw.

Exhausted but well sated, she was held against him. Their bodies were hot, damp from exertion. She smiled and toyed with the unruly locks of hair that fell on his forehead. "Do you ever run out of energy? I can't move. But I'm so happy."

"Darlin', you can't imagine how happy I am," he said, running his hand lightly over her bare back. "And if I have some extra energy, it's because I'm with you and you tease it out of me. You're beautiful. I want you here in my arms the rest of the day and night. Don't get out of bed."

She smiled. "Ridiculous man."

"I used to give you marbles or chocolate to bribe you to get you to do what I wanted. How can I bribe you to stay in this bed with me all day?"

"Promise me we can touch and feel and kiss all day," she answered in a sultry whisper while she ran her tongue over his ear.

He groaned, crushed her against his chest and kissed her hard. She wrapped her arms around him to kiss him in return.

Finally, she pushed against him, putting some space between them. He gave her a questioning look and she placed her hand on his jaw. "Hold it, cowboy. You're going to wear me to a frazzle and I think we missed some eating along the way."

"I'd like to eat you up," he whispered, kissing her throat.

"Whoa. Do you hear my stomach with a rebuttal? I would like to have dinner. We have been in this bed almost the whole time since we got here and my stomach is definitely hungry."

"Let me feel and see what I think," he said, rolling her over beside him so he could lightly rub her stomach.

When his hand dipped a little too low, she slipped out of bed and walked completely naked to the bathroom.

As she showered, she thought about Gabe. In a few days she would be engaged to him. And in a few days she would be telling her family. She dreaded it, because doing so would cause a fire-storm of arguments.

She refused to let those fears bring her down, so she turned her thoughts to Gabe and their love-making that only made her want him more than ever. She was lost in memories of the past few hours. Because she was wrapped in euphoria from making love it was hard to know the extent of her feelings and how much they had shifted after becoming intimate with him. All she really did know was that she couldn't wait for tonight, when she got to share his bed and do it all again.

It was Tuesday when they returned to Dallas. Gabe drove and listened to Meg babbling about their plans. She was excited, bubbling with so much eagerness she could barely sit still. She'd called home and talked for almost an hour to her mother on Sunday, so her mother knew she'd been visiting Gabe's ranch and they were return-ing to Dallas today so she could go to work.

Filled with mixed feelings, Gabe thought about them as he drove. Early in the morning he had stirred while Meg was still asleep. He still wanted to look at her constantly because she was gorgeous. That wasn't all that'd had him staring at her while she slept. She was the most exciting woman to kiss and the most sensual and sexy in bed. Just thinking about it now could get him aroused and he took a deep breath, trying to focus on what she was saying and on watching the road as he drove.

He had a strange feeling that he might be getting in over his head. He hadn't ever had a woman in his life like her. She came into his life like a whirlwind and he suspected she might leave it the same way—with his life in a shambles when she was gone. He didn't want commitment and he couldn't commit to anything with her because they really weren't compatible when it came to lifestyles.

Frustrated when he hit some traffic, he wished he wasn't in the car. This long drive was ridiculous. She just needed to get on a plane and find out how easy it was to fly to Dallas from his ranch or to the ranch from Dallas, but she wouldn't fly.

She had turned his life inside out. He had never

missed anyone after breaking up with them but he had mixed feelings about telling Meg good-bye at the end of the month. After these past few days he would miss her in his bed and in his life, but he would be glad to get his life back. And get back to ranching. He had taken her to see his prize bull yesterday. She had taken one quick look, shuddered and told him that was all she wanted to see of his livestock.

Despite that, for right now, he wanted every moment he could get with her and he wanted her in his bed and in his arms. She dazzled him in so many ways. She had certainly changed as she had grown up. She was so much more con-fident, self-sufficient, and she had a zest for life that amazed him. He couldn't imagine her fam-ily trying to push her into marriage, but he could understand Justin wanting to marry her.

Tonight Gabe wanted to do something special. It wasn't a real engagement, and tonight wouldn't be a real proposal, but she deserved something special. Something that was just between them and had nothing to do with the goofy fake en-gagement. Something that told her it was great to be with her again even though he wasn't totally thrilled to admit that she excited him more than any other woman he had ever known.

Her looks still blew him away. She didn't seem to give them much thought, but that didn't change her beauty. He suspected at some point in time she would revert back to her grade school hairdo and drop the makeup. But he would be attracted to her no matter which way she dressed.

Because of their differences in lifestyles and outlooks, if she hadn't been desperate for his help, she never would have gone out with him. That might have been mutual because he wouldn't have asked her out, either. Funny how that worked out, he thought.

Soon they would part, but before they did, he wanted to make her happy. Starting with tonight.

She poked his thigh with her finger. "Are you listening to me?"

Amused, he grinned. "Sorry. I was thinking about this morning in bed and thinking about you. What were you telling me?"

"For just a few minutes, get your mind out of the bedroom."

"I'll try, but it isn't easy after some time in there with you."

She smiled and blew him a kiss, making him laugh.

"I was just reviewing the plan to announce our engagement this week," she told him.

"I want you to be absolutely sure that's still what you want because it will upset your folks."

"Stop worrying. I want the announcement."

He glanced at her and she smiled sweetly while nodding at him, making him laugh again.

Her car was at her house, so he dropped her there and got out to walk her to her door.

"You don't need to come with me," she said, stepping out of his car.

"Oh, yes, I do," he answered, taking her arm and inhaling her exotic new perfume.

She unlocked her back door and they stepped into her tiny entryway. He closed the door and turned to take her into his arms. Her brown eyes widened as she looked up in obvious surprise, which lasted one second before her arms wrapped around his waist and she gave in to his kiss.

She was soft, sweet, giving him the sexiest

kisses of his life, and he wanted to carry her to bed now. He raised his head. "Go to work later."

Her eyes were heavy lidded and she tightened her arm around his waist and pulled him close again. His mouth covered hers and as he kissed her, he picked her up, carrying her to a bedroom.

It was three hours before he stood at her back door again. "I'll pick you up at seven and tonight you're staying at my house."

All she wore was a blue bath towel, which she pulled tight around her as she nodded.

"You look too good to leave," he said.

"You go. You're taking my whole day and I have to go to my office. Goodbye."

He wiped his brow and took one more long look at her. "If you drop that towel, I won't be able to leave."

"I'm not dropping it and you go now. The door will lock behind you." She turned and left, stepping out of sight through a door into her kitchen.

He left and went to his car to drive to his house. He wanted her constantly. He expected that to wear off as it always did, but right now, he couldn't stop thinking about her and wanting to be with her.

At his house he fished out the fake ring she had given him and turned it in his hand. It was a beautiful ring and at a glance looked impressive and real. Yesterday he had phoned his florist and ordered flowers sent to her office so the flowers would be there when she arrived today. If Justin dropped into her office, he would see the flowers and probably find out who had sent them.

Gabe wanted to surprise her about tonight and had made reservations at an elegant steak house. On short notice he'd needed to call in some favors to get a reservation. The place had great steaks, the perfect ambience and there would be people they knew who would see them together—the essential requirement for Meg to consider the evening a success. He smiled and placed the ring back in the velvet box.

Soon Meg would be gone out of his life. He wasn't ready for that yet and hoped he could talk her into continuing to date for a while longer.

He suspected she would not. She was afraid of falling in love with the wrong guy and he assumed the minute this engagement was over, she would disappear out of his life.

If she did, he would have to live with that. Sooner or later he knew they would say goodbye, but he'd rather keep her around longer. She was incredible in bed—instantly responsive and eager, filled with energy, wanting him and trying to please him as much as he pleased her.

He left to go to his office, the tall building he shared with Cade in their commercial real estate business, but on the way he made a stop to get a present for her for the evening.

For the rest of the day he had the hardest time concentrating on work. All he could think about was Meg. He couldn't wait to get her to dinner, give her the ring and then get her back to the privacy of his house, where he wanted to make love to her all night long. Their time together was limited and he intended to make the most of it before they said goodbye.

At the end of the month or whenever they parted, would it bother him to tell her goodbye? It never had with anyone else, so maybe it wouldn't with Meg. Besides, she had a way of bouncing back into his life.

He put away his papers, closed up and left his office. While he couldn't wait to see her, this fake engagement was playing hell with his life. But it had given him Meg in his bed and that was definitely worth all the trouble she had caused him. How much more delight and trouble would tonight bring?

Nine

Meg heard her doorbell and rushed through her small house. She glanced in the mirror at herself again, looking at a red dress with a full skirt that came to her knees. Her sleeveless top had a vee neckline. She wore high-heeled red sandals and her hair fell loosely on either side of her face. Tonight she would get engaged to marry Gabe. The thought took her breath away even though she was totally aware it was a fake. After tonight she and Gabe would be bound together in the eyes of her family and the town. She wavered between excitement, even though it was fake, and worry that it would draw her closer to him, closer to falling in love if she wasn't already doing that. They were not suited for each other and neither one could change their lifestyle. She couldn't suddenly start flying and loving it, riding on his Harley—what a thought. She would be terrified. Gabe complicated her life in one way, but he had brought her freedom in another and he was a great guy. Whatever their future, tonight excited her and she couldn't wait.

She opened the door and drew a deep breath as she looked up at Gabe in his broad-brimmed black hat, his navy Western suit and tailor-made white shirt. He looked so handsome, she wanted to pull him inside, close the door, step into his arms and make love all night long.

Instead, she had to stick to the program they had agreed on for the evening. She smiled at him. "Hi, my handsome, irresistible cowboy," she said in a sultry voice.

"Oh, damn. I'm taking you to dinner when all I want to do is take you to bed."

Should she tell him she had the same thought? Should she tell him she wanted the same thing?

His eyes were practically singeing her skin as they raked her over from head to toe.

His voice turned huskier when he said, "You know, darlin', we can skip dinner—"

She interrupted before he went any further. "No, we can't. We're going to stick to the script for tonight. We go out to eat where we can be seen and you propose. I accept and we have a fake engagement. We go see my parents and show them the ring. I call Justin and then we're free to do whatever you want, my strong cowboy."

"I'm not sure I can wait that long."

She laughed. "Yes, you can. Let's go get this show on the road. This is the night doors fly open and I walk out of Justin's life forever. We're both better off."

"I have to agree with that one. I'd hate to have to bribe someone to marry me." He pulled out his phone. "Stand still. I want one picture of you looking so beautiful, and then one with me." He took them quickly and put away his phone. "I'll pull those out on cold, empty nights and remember what fun I had with you."

"Oh, right. Like you have so many empty nights." She smiled at him, then locked up and started toward the car.

He took her arm and wrapped it around his. "Darlin', I'll be counting the minutes until I can get you in my arms and out of that gorgeous red dress."

"You really do have a one-track mind, don't you?" But she couldn't deny his words thrilled her.

He gave her a devilish smile as he held the car door open for her. "Don't you love it?"

"What I love is that bouquet you sent me. It was beautiful, gigantic. The flowers almost fill up my office. Roses, tulips, daisies, big white lilies, gladiola, baby's breath and freesias. And right in the middle of all the beautiful flowers was a new brown teddy bear," she said, laughing as he got in beside her. "That was the part that really got to me. That cute little bear. I'll thank you properly when we get home."

"Excellent. That's what I aimed for. That and to help get a message to Justin if he came to your office."

"They said he did drop by and he did see the bouquet. He left and never came back or called. I think he has the message and is acting on it. You darling man," she said, blowing him kisses.

He pretended to catch them and pull them close to his heart, his face taking on an exaggerated moue of passion while his eyebrows jumped.

She couldn't help but laugh.

"Gabe, you're still fun. I always thought you were amusing when we were kids. You still are. Handsome, too," she said. Actually, she'd go so far as to say he was the most handsome man she knew. As they pulled away from her street, she let her gaze run over his profile. Oh, yes, he was that. And she couldn't deny she wanted the evening to be over and to be home, his place or hers, and in his arms.

"I could say the same about you, Meg," he said. "I just had no idea the talents you would have when you grew up. I should have taken you out way before now."

"You wouldn't have had the same results, so don't fill yourself with regrets."

"It's those 'results' I'm looking forward to."

As he slowed for a light, he shot her a smoldering glance that nearly set her on fire. "If not for your plan I would turn this car around and take you home and spend the evening the best way possible." He grabbed the gearshift.

She stilled his hand. "But you're not going to do that, because this is the most essential part of my plan."

Reluctantly, he kept the car in Drive and moved forward.

Minutes later they were pulling into the best restaurant in town.

"Here we are," Gabe said, turning onto a winding drive on broad, landscaped grounds. Ponds with fountains flanked the road, as well as tall oaks and willows.

Twinkling lights covered the red crepe myrtles at the entrance with the sun still above the horizon. A valet took the car and Meg entered on Gabe's arm.

It was dim inside, and she heard a violin playing in the background. The maître d' met them and led them to a table overlooking a sloping backyard of more tall trees, statues and fountains, with a creek running across the green grounds.

Candlelight flickered in the hurricane lamp on the table beside a crystal vase with four red and pink roses.

It was perfect. The place, the setting, the man. If she ever really did get engaged, this was the place she wanted it to happen.

For the first time, she felt a niggling pain in the area around her heart. *Remember, Meg, it's all pretend.*

"Give me your hand," he said, placing his hand on the gold linen tablecloth.

She forced a smile and looked up at him as she gave him her hand.

He tilted his head as he watched her. "Why the solemn look?"

"You're too observant for my own good, you know that?" Then again, nobody knew her as well as Gabe. She should have known she wouldn't be able to keep her feelings a secret from him. "It's nothing really. Just that…well, someday you're going to do this for real and she's going to be a lucky woman. You're a nice guy, Gabe."

"Thank you. But you sound as if you think it'll never happen for you. I promise you that someday a man will be asking to marry you for real. Darlin', you'll have so many great guys wanting to take you out the minute I get out of this picture. In less than a month you'll be having the time of your life." He smiled at her.

But she didn't smile back.

Gabe ordered champagne and when their waiter left, Gabe raised his crystal flute. "Here's to success in your endeavor that brought us back together for a very wonderful, unforgettable time."

"Thank you." She touched his flute with hers as she looked into his blue eyes in the flickering candlelight. Their glasses had a melodic ring when they touched.

Still watching him, sharing the moment, she sipped the bubbly, pale yellow champagne. A moment later she made a toast of her own. "Here's to you, Gabe Callahan, for being the cowboy to the lady's rescue, even though you didn't ride in on a white horse." As she sipped her champagne, once again she felt a squeeze to her heart. She had no future of any sort with Gabe. This had been a task to accomplish and he had nearly accomplished it, and they really were almost finished. The month would soon be over and they would go their separate ways. Gabe was great in so many ways, but he was definitely no more the man for her than she was the woman for him.

They touched glasses again and she took another sip as Gabe reached down and pulled a long black box out of his jacket pocket. It was tied with a blue silk bow. He placed it in the middle of the table.

"I know we have things we'll do tonight while we're here. This isn't one you had scheduled in. This one I planned." He swallowed and looked up at her. "This has been a special time, Meg. We've been the best of friends and together off and on through the years. Now we're not only friends, we're intimate, and that's a change to a deeper relationship that holds more importance. To make sure you'll remember the moment and know that it was important to me, here's a keepsake for you. When you wear that, think of me."

"But, Gabe, you sent flowers and another teddy bear. I don't need more presents."

He pushed the box closer to her. "Please."

Curious, she picked it up and untied the blue silk bow and opened the box. She gasped as she looked at the necklace resting on black velvet. Small diamonds formed the necklace, leading to a pendant that was a large sparkling diamond surrounded by alternating diamonds and emeralds.

She looked up at him. "Gabe, this is spectacular. It's beautiful."

"It's for you, and when we're home tonight I'll put it on you."

"I can't wait. I've never had anything like this. It's magnificent." She reached out and squeezed his hand. "Thank you."

"Whatever the future brings, Meg, we have a history that goes way back and you've been important in my life. You got me through some rough times. I wanted you to have something special."

"It's fabulous, Gabe. Thank you." She glanced down at the necklace and then back up to him. "I can't do much more than keep saying 'thank you' as long as we're in public here."

"You'll get your chance to thank me when we get back to my place. You can wait till then for me to put your necklace on you. Or you can come over here and sit on my lap and I'll fasten it for you."

Smiling, she shook her head. She didn't trust herself to sit on his lap right now. She gazed at him, taking in every inch of his beautiful face, thinking of how exciting he was, how good he was to her. Why did they have to be so opposite in lifestyles?

Their waiter came to take orders and as soon as he left, she turned to Gabe.

Raising her flute, she gazed into his blue eyes. "Here's a big thank-you to my very best friend for all my life." Smiling, she touched her flute to his and sipped her champagne as their waiter brought green salads on crystal plates.

The meal, like the place, was perfection. They both had rib eyes, sweet potatoes with pecans, and fluffy biscuits drizzled with honey.

It was after dinner as they sipped Irish coffee that Gabe got out another smaller box tied with a red satin ribbon.

"The time has come," he said after he glanced around the dining room. "You said you wanted a lot of people to see us so it gets back to Justin—well, watch this move. I'm betting this will blow up social media and Justin will see it within the hour."

She smiled, watching Gabe get up. As if on cue, the violin player strolled in their direction, playing a sweet ballad. He stopped several feet away from Gabe, who handed the box to her. As he did, she looked into his blue eyes and her heart pounded even though these actions were following a script she'd written.

Suddenly she saw this as a big moment, and one that made her feel as if her life were about to change, all because of the next few minutes.

"Open your present."

She smiled at the drama Gabe was adding to their plan. The quiet restaurant had grown even quieter and she realized they had an audience. He was right. Comments and pictures would fly on social media.

She untied the ribbon, glancing up at Gabe, whose blue eyes twinkled with mischief. She raised the lid, expecting to see the ring she had purchased. Instead a smaller black box was inside the bigger box. Unbuttoning his jacket, Gabe took that box as she looked up at him expectantly. He opened the box, tossed the lid on the table, removed the dazzling fake diamond she had selected herself and knelt on one knee in front of her to take her hand. She looked at his well-shaped hands as they held hers and she felt her heart seize.

The violin player stepped closer, still playing sweetly.

"Megan Louise Aldridge," Gabe said loudly enough for his voice to carry, "will you make me, Gabriel Callahan, the luckiest man in the world? Will you marry me?"

She couldn't help it. For this one moment in time, she suddenly wished the diamond was real, this proposal was real. Gabe was her best friend. He was the most exciting lover possible. He was handsome and intelligent, caring and kind. For just an instant, she wished that his words were sincere and their lives would be joined forever. Wished she would be Mrs. Gabe Callahan. She saw it all playing out in front of her. The wedding, and a lifetime of happiness.

Then, just as quickly, the lovely images faded away.

She could never have a permanent relationship with Gabe. She could never live with a wild risk-taker, never love someone whose safety she would be in constant fear for.

Then she realized Gabe, as well as their audience, was waiting for her answer.

"Yes. Oh, yes, Gabe," she said, as he slipped the ring on her finger. He stood up, holding her wrist as she rose, and drew her to him to kiss her. Their audience clapped while the violin player broke into a snappy rendition of Mendelssohn's "Wedding March."

She barely heard it, because though the proposal hadn't been real, his kiss was. She held him as tightly as he held her and for a few seconds she forgot where she was or what was happening. All she knew was she was in Gabe's arms and he was kissing her as thoroughly as she was kissing him.

When she stepped back, she met his gaze. The

spell was broken by the resounding applause and a couple of whistles. The violinist continued playing "Wedding March" as Gabe held her hand, and they bowed and smiled at the diners before sitting down again and letting quiet return to the restaurant.

"Gabe, let's go. You've already paid the waiter. I want to leave."

"You're not going to get to leave for a little while longer," he said. "Here come some people we know, and they probably want to congratulate us. Let's just hope everyone in the restaurant doesn't decide to wish us well."

"Oh, my gracious," she said, smiling as friends came to congratulate them.

The minute the last person left, Meg picked up her purse and present and the boxes. "Gabe, we have to get out of here. We've posed for pictures, and people took pictures of us when you proposed. There were probably people who even got videos of it. Our families will know about this. Justin will know before we can tell anyone."

"This worked out to be a little more of a response than I had envisioned in this quiet, staid, expensive restaurant. I'm ready, darlin'." He stood up, came around to pull out her chair. "They're probably all thinking we're going somewhere to make love. How I wish."

"Come on, let's go."

They walked out together and as soon as she was in the car, she called her mother. "Mom, can Gabe and I come by the house? I have some news."

Meg listened a moment. "We'll see you in about half an hour," she said, thinking about how long it would take. "See you then." She ended the call.

"They hadn't heard?" Gabe asked.

"No. My folks aren't on social media. Let's go tell them we're engaged."

"I hope your dad doesn't slug me."

"My father would never do any such thing."

Gabe smiled. "I really didn't think he would, but he is not going to like this and your mom isn't, either. And I hope it doesn't give your poor grandparents fainting spells when you call them."

"Stop being a pessimist."

Gabe shook his head. "I know one thing. Your folks won't hug me and say, 'Welcome to the family.'"

* * *

While Gabe watched traffic, he dreaded facing her folks and announcing they were engaged. Even though he'd agreed to this situation, it went against living an honest life. Meg's folks should never have tried to push her into a loveless marriage. She was too loving and full of life to settle for a guy who was marrying her solely to get a promotion in his dad's firm.

He heard her phone ring and glanced over at her as she checked the screen.

"Well, Justin must have seen a picture of us because this call is from him. I might as well talk to him about it now."

Gabe wondered if Justin had already heard about his proposal and was angry about what was happening, but he didn't care to hear her conversation.

"Seriously?" she gasped. "Seriously? You mean that?" She sounded so shocked Gabe glanced at her to see her staring at him wide-eyed with her mouth hanging open and her face pale.

Wondering if someone had died in Justin's family, Gabe signaled and once again got off the freeway and into a residential area where he parked.

"When did this happen?" she asked.

Now Gabe wished he had told her to put the call on speaker. Something had happened to someone in Justin's family. Hopefully Justin was all right himself.

"I'm shocked. I wish you the very best. I really mean that. I hope you're so happy and that everything good comes your way."

Gabe stared at her, trying to guess what Justin was going to do that had her wishing him the best. His curiosity grew and he wondered what had happened and how it would affect her.

"Thank you, Justin. That's nice of you. Yes, we'll do that sometime. Tell your family hello and I'm thrilled for you, for all of you." She nodded as Justin must have been talking. "Sure. I'll see you then for sure. Congratulations. I'm so happy for both of you. Goodbye."

She turned to Gabe, but he wondered whether she saw him or not.

"I can't believe what he just told me," she said, sounding dazed. She focused on Gabe and he waited patiently. "Justin is engaged. He's getting married. He's engaged to Pamela Gatersen. They went together all their senior year in college and then went to different law schools. They just got back together and it was a whirlwind courtship and everything worked out perfectly. He sounded as if he had won the lottery. They'll have a Christmas wedding and travel around the world for a honeymoon."

Gabe knew of her. "Her dad owns Gatersen Equipment, which is a nationwide company—heavy-duty stuff, tractors, backhoes, trucks. Hon, she probably has way more money in her family than you do in yours and that seems to be highly important to Justin."

"I'm in shock. I didn't expect that. He sounded so happy to tell me."

"I imagine he is because you've given him grief. He must have wished you well, though. I heard you thank him."

"He did. He said, 'Best wishes for a happy life with your cowboy,'" she said, smiling at Gabe.

"Think he heard about my proposal?"

She nodded. "Yes, he did. He has us to thank for getting him out of a loveless marriage."

She looked at Gabe. "This lets you off the hook, too. We don't have to announce our fake engagement now. You can have your life back, and peace and quiet."

"Don't be so hasty. We're going to see your folks. What about them?"

"Right. I'll call and tell Mom about Justin and say that was what I was going to tell her, but it isn't necessary to drop by. Let me call them now."

She made the call and as soon as she finished, she turned to him. "That was quick and easy, and Mom is happy for Justin, and for me since that was what I wanted. I'll talk to my dad next time I'm home."

Gabe took her hand in his, and he looked her deep in the eyes. "Come home with me tonight, Meg. Don't change tonight."

Before she could answer, Meg felt as if she'd been hit by a truck. Out of nowhere the thought entered her head. She couldn't believe she hadn't realized the problem right away.

"Oh, Gabe. What about your proposal in the restaurant?"

He shook his head. "Damn, that backfired, I guess. Justin's engaged and so am I."

"No, you're not. I'll just tell people we aren't getting married. I can tell my friends that my folks were pressuring me into a marriage and you did that to get me out of being pushed into one. It'll blow over with tomorrow's news. And your family already knows what the situation is. Mine might hear the rumors, but I'll tell them not to worry."

"True enough. So that's that, I guess." Gabe started up the car and pulled back onto the freeway.

"I think I owe Justin one for getting me back with you for a little while. It's been fun hanging out again, Meg."

She was deep in thought about this being her last night with him. Gabe had come back into her life and been all the great things he had been when they were kids, plus all the wonderful things he was now.

She twisted the big dazzling ring on her finger.

She smiled at him and placed her hand on his thigh, feeling his warmth through his trousers. Once again, she was struck by what a kind man Gabe had grown up to be.

She agreed to go to his house. Gabe was right. There was no reason to change that part of their plans.

Once he closed his front door behind her, he took her into his arms to kiss her.

"I want to put on my necklace," she told him when she stepped away.

"Sure," he said, pausing. "Get it out and I'll put it on you."

She opened the box to look at the dazzling necklace again. "Gabe, this is magnificent. I've never had anything like it. It's so beautiful."

"Good. I'm glad you like it." He picked it up and stepped behind her, scooping up her long locks to lift them out of the way. "Hold your hair up for me," he said. He bent to fasten the clasp and the safety and then he trailed kisses on her nape.

Gasping, she closed her eyes and stood for a moment, relishing his kisses before she dropped her hair and turned, putting her arms around Gabe's neck, standing on tiptoe and kissing him.

His strong arms banded her and held her tightly while he kissed her in return and made her heart pound. She could hardly believe this was the night she would tell him goodbye. After tonight Gabe would disappear out of her life again and she wouldn't see him, except for possibly some social events around Dallas. The knowledge hurt and she wondered how important he had become to her. Had she fallen in love with him? She didn't have to search deeply to know the answer was yes. And she was going to hurt badly when she told him goodbye.

Ten

Running her hands over Gabe's body, Meg wanted to kiss every inch of him. In her heart she was certain this was goodbye. There was no reason to stay now and every time they made love it bound her more closely to him and made him more important to her.

The longer she stayed, the more difficult it would be to leave. And maybe the more in love with him she would be.

Regardless, she wanted tonight with Gabe.

But what if he asked her to stay longer? Would she stay?

She couldn't. If she did, she would never want

to leave him. Gabe had been her best friend as a child and growing up—he was still her best friend in too many ways.

Running her hands over him, she pushed away his jacket and let it fall. She twisted the buttons on his tailored white shirt free, taking out the gold cuff links he wore and dropping them in his trouser pocket while they continued to kiss.

She looked up at him. "I'm going to miss you."

"I'm not gone," he said. "Not yet." He tangled his fingers in her hair, tugged lightly to tilt her head back and then kissed her, his tongue stroking her lower lip, the corners of her mouth, before going deep with slow thrusts that made her hot, made her want him.

She unfastened his trousers to free him. Unbuckling his belt, she pushed away the trousers and briefs and he stepped out of them, yanking off his boots and socks.

He had already pulled down the zipper at the back of her dress and it fell around her ankles. He held her away from him while his gaze roamed over her and his hands followed.

"You're so incredibly beautiful. I want to look

at you and touch you all night. I want you in my arms, your naked body against mine all night. I want everything, Meg. You'll never know how much I want you."

As he looked at her, she studied him, tingling at the sight of his strong, virile male body. He was fully aroused, ready to love. He was tan, fit, all hard muscles and flat planes. She knelt to caress him, running her hands between his legs along his inner thighs and taking his thick shaft in hand to stroke and run her tongue over him.

He tangled his fingers in her hair again, groaning quietly, his throbbing manhood dark and hard.

With a harsh cry, he slipped his hands beneath her arms to pull her slowly to her feet. She rubbed against him while his hands roamed over her and she showered kisses over him. Her hands traveled across his belly and down his legs, moving in feathery caresses all over him.

Finally, he picked her up and carried her to the nearest bedroom, tossing back covers and placing her on the bed, coming down to hold her close.

She loved him with abandon, kissing him and

knowing it was the last time, memorizing how he looked and felt, and exciting him until he shook.

She did everything she could to pleasure him, to give him a night he would remember, lovemaking that would be important to him and intimacy that he couldn't forget. Her hands were everywhere over him, touching, stroking and teasing while she showered kisses on him, rubbing and caressing him and letting him do what he wanted to her.

With a groan, he stilled her hands and moved between her legs, pausing to put on a condom before he lowered himself and entered her in one thrust.

She locked her legs around him and held him while they kissed. They drew out their lovemaking, rising to a brink and falling back, then rising again until she could take no more. She gasped and clung to him, crying out when his control went and they climaxed together, hard and fast.

Exhausted and euphoric, they held each other. He stroked her lightly, his hand caressing her, moving over her. "You're marvelous, every inch of you," he whispered, showering light kisses on her temple, her cheek, her ear and her throat. He gently combed long strands of hair from her face with his fingers.

"Meg, I want you to stay. Stay this month."

While she felt a pang and longing enveloped her, she shook her head.

"I can't do that, Gabe. I'd be so in love I could never leave. The month would end and we would be right back where we are now."

"Stay this week then. That's not long and you won't fall in love in the few days left in the week."

She ran her hands over him. She lay pressed against him, her leg thrown over his while her hands continued to roam over him. She couldn't tell him that she was already in love with him. "No. You have your life and your things you like to do. I have my work that I need to get back to. I can't be casual about lovemaking. Physical love for me is still all tied up with my emotions and my heart."

"You always were sentimental. I guess that's why you still have that silly brown bear I gave you so long ago."

"I suppose." She turned on her side to face him.

"I want you to know that this has been special, Gabe. You did a good job and saved the day for me. You gave me that beautiful necklace. You're the one who should get a present because you did just what I asked."

"This is my present, Meg, holding you in my arms, loving you all night, kissing you. Will you go to dinner with me next Friday?"

She looked down a moment while she twisted her fingers in his chest hair. Finally, she shook her head. "No, I don't think I should, because you'll want me to come back here and sleep with you and I'm not going to continue to do that."

"If you change your mind, call me," he said, looking solemn.

"I will. I haven't looked in the mirror at my beautiful necklace that I'm still wearing. I'm going to do that, then shower and get dressed and go home to Downly. We'll say goodbye."

"I'm going to miss you."

"No, you won't. You'll find a pretty lady who will be fun and you'll forget all about me."

She rolled over, wrapping the top sheet around her and stepping out of bed to go shower. "See you in a few minutes." She left, letting out her breath. She wanted to say yes to every question he asked her. She wanted to stay the rest of the month. She wanted to stay tonight. But anything more she did with him would bind her to him just that much more. She was in love with him. In the past it had been friendship and that had been all, but this time together had been different from the moment they first kissed. She wondered if she'd fallen in love with him right then.

She dressed in jeans, a red knit shirt and boots. When she stepped into the hall he was waiting. He crossed the hall to her and put his hands on her shoulders. "I don't want you to go. Meg, I want you to stay. At least stay tonight."

A knot formed in her throat and she took a deep breath. A longing to say yes tore at her and she hurt. "I can't stay with you. I'll fall in love, and that would just mean heartbreak because you won't want any kind of real commitment. Even if you did, I can't live with your lifestyle."

His jaw firmed and a cold look filled his eyes. "Dammit, Meg. I'm me. I love my life and doing the things I do. I make a lot of money raising and breeding and selling those rodeo bulls and my cattle. I fly often. I like fast cars. I live and enjoy life."

"Oh, Gabe," she cried, throwing her arms around his neck and crying, sobbing in his arms as he embraced her and held her close. When she could, she stopped and raised her head, telling him the words she never thought she'd speak to him.

"I'm probably already in love with you. But I know I don't love the way you live. I can't deal with it. I don't want to fall in love or be in love with someone who will be killed doing something wild and unnecessary like my brother was. It hurts too badly to lose someone you love, and you've been a part of my life since I was little. I couldn't bear it if something happened to you. And I don't want to be afraid every time you leave the house."

No matter how much she hurt and couldn't stop crying, she couldn't move in with him. She had to walk away, for all those reasons.

Looking grim, he wrapped his arms around her and held her while she clung to him and cried.

When she finally managed to get control, she wiped her eyes and looked up at him. "I guess there isn't much else to say."

"I can't change completely, Meg. I'm me and I have to stay that way."

"I can't change either, Gabe."

"Is this our first fight?" he asked. She guessed he was trying to lighten the moment, but a muscle worked in his jaw and his blue eyes had darkened. While she knew he was hurt and angry, she couldn't move in with him. She hurt now, but it would be nothing compared to moving in with him and then having to say goodbye when she left—or when something terrible happened to him.

"It might be our first fight," she replied, but she couldn't smile because she hurt too badly. "We never fought as kids. You were always my best friend and I guess you still are."

"Good luck, Meg. I'll miss you more than you can possibly imagine."

"I'll have to get the rest of my things from your ranch. I'll do that soon, or you bring them to Dallas and I'll pick them up here." She looked up at him. "Thank you, Gabe, for my beautiful necklace. Thank you for everything you did."

"I told you, I wouldn't have missed this for the world. We've known each other forever, but in some ways, you're new in my life." He took her hand. "If you can change your mind, I'm here. Call me anytime, because you'll always be welcome back."

"Thank you, Gabe." She stood on tiptoe to kiss him and he held her tightly, leaning over her and kissing her until she was ready to head back to the bedroom with him. But she knew she had to go.

She hurt all over and was icy cold, shivering, hating every step she took away from him, but she couldn't change how she felt and neither could he.

He watched her drive away and with every bit of distance, she felt as if she was losing a chunk of her heart. She saw him in the rearview mirror as she went down his drive. He stood with his hands on his hips watching her go. She had fallen in love with him and she was leaving her heart behind. How long would it take to get over him? She wondered if she'd ever get over him because she felt as if he was the man she would love the rest of her life.

Tears filled her eyes and fell on her cheeks. She wanted to be in his arms, in his bed. She wanted his cheer and his laughter and his fun. She wanted his friendship that had always been so important to her.

It was over and she would just have to get over him someway. If she thought about all the wild things he did, maybe she wouldn't miss him so much.

She drove home, called the office to tell them she wouldn't be in and then threw herself on the bed, hugging both brown bears as she cried.

Gabe watched Meg drive away and he felt as if he was losing something important in his life. He liked women, had affairs, broke up, said good-bye, remained friends—all of that. But he hadn't ever hurt when he had said goodbye. Not once in his life. And he'd definitely never hurt like he did now.

It was ridiculous. How could she mean that

much to him and make him want to be with her? Sometimes she was pure trouble. She didn't like his lifestyle. She was scared of his bulls, scared of his bull riding. She didn't like his fast car and she couldn't bear his motorcycle. Why in the world would he miss her?

She was his best friend in a lot of ways, but he had brothers, a half brother, other best friends. Meg had him in knots half the time. He had assumed she was bringing trouble to his doorstep the first day she showed up and he had been right. His life hadn't been the same since and it wasn't going to swing back to the peace and quiet he'd had before she arrived.

Could it be—

No, he couldn't be in love. He stared down his driveway. He could still see her driving away and it hurt to watch her go.

If she had captured his heart, what the hell would he do about it? He turned and walked back into his house that seemed silent and lifeless. He had never felt that way about his home, either. It was as if she had sailed into his life, turned it upside down, stolen his heart, melted him in bed and then driven right out of his life again, leaving him in shambles and feeling empty and lost.

"Dammit, Meg," he said, frowning. He was going to the ranch, would get her big bag and bring it back here for her to pick up. Maybe he would see her again when she picked it up. Maybe he could even get her to stay for a while.

That thought wasn't at all like him. What the hell had she done to him?

He refused to believe he could be in love with her. That would just be another disaster in his life caused by Meg. He didn't want to give up his way of life, his fun car, his planes. Speaking of his planes… He called to get one ready. Instead of driving to the ranch, he'd fly—and try to get her out of his system. He'd lived without her for years. Surely he could do so again.

"Oh, right," he said aloud. That was before they had kissed or gone to bed together. Her kisses were the most dazzling, bone-melting, instantly arousing kisses ever. And making love with her was the best.

Are you sure you're not in love with her?

"No!" he said emphatically. At least, he hoped

to hell he wasn't. If he was in love—heaven forbid—she'd wreck his life. And she wouldn't ever marry him because of the way he lived. He'd managed to live his entire life and not once fall in love. His first time couldn't—wouldn't—be with Meg. That would be disastrous. Sort of. He thought again about kissing her and making love and in minutes he was hard and wanting her.

If this was love, then love was hell.

He nearly ripped off his clothes and changed, then closed up his house.

If he wanted Meg in his life permanently, he'd have to get rid of his bulls—a fine living there. He'd also have to ditch his planes—she didn't know he had two—also ditch his fast car and his Harley. If he married her, which was impossible, she probably wouldn't want him to go out in the rain or snow.

"Damn," he said aloud. It wasn't really living if you were scared of your own shadow. He knew her feelings were 90 percent because of losing her brother, but Hank wouldn't have wanted her to go through life scared of a lot of things.

Gabe got into his car to go to the airport and

fly to his ranch. He was going to get her out of his life, out of his thoughts. He just couldn't be in love. Even if she accepted his lifestyle—which she never would—he didn't want to be tied down. That would mean the same woman for the rest of his life. He thought about Meg being with him all the time, in his bed every night, and he broke out in a sweat again.

He swore again as he got out his phone to call her, changed his mind and put it away. They had said goodbye and he was going to leave it that way.

He should have barricaded himself in his house the day he saw her coming up his drive to ask for his help.

Since he hadn't done that, he'd think about other women who could cure him of Meg. Mentally he ran through a list of beauties he'd been interested in. That lasted about thirty seconds before Meg returned to his thoughts. He remembered how she had looked when she had opened the door and he had faced a stunning blonde that he hadn't even recognized. He groaned, and wondered if she had changed his life irrevocably. He looked down at his speedometer and took his foot off the gas. He was going faster than even he thought his car should be driven.

He needed to get a grip and stop thinking about her. Even if he was in love, it couldn't be serious and she would fade into the background soon. She had to, because right now his life was hell without her.

Meg tried everything. She threw herself into her business, working harder and longer in order to be so exhausted she would sleep at night instead of lying awake thinking about Gabe. But that didn't work. She missed him. Without him, she felt a huge void in her life. She was beginning to think she wasn't ever going to get over him.

He had called and told her he had her bag at his Dallas home. But she had appointments and schedules to keep, customers who wanted landscaping plans, and she hadn't picked up the bag yet.

She was trying to forget him while at the same time she wanted to see him again. But she felt that when she went to get her bag it would be the last time she would see Gabe, and she couldn't face that.

She looked at the picture a friend had sent her, the one she'd shoved into a pile on her desk. It was a picture of Gabe in the restaurant on his knee, proposing to her.

The picture made her laugh, but it also made her long to be with him and remember all the fun they'd had together, plus the hot sex. Just thinking about that made her want his strong arms around her. She threw the photo into the desk drawer.

After he called twice about her bag, offering to bring it to her, she decided she should go get it. She made arrangements to take time from the office, called Gabe and finally set a time to pick it up on Wednesday. It had been a week since she had last seen him but it seemed as if it had been months.

Wednesday morning, she wound up his drive to his Dallas house and saw him waiting on the porch for her arrival. He was in a white shirt without a tie, charcoal slacks and his black boots. Her pulse sped up as he came out to meet her.

"Hi, come in. You don't have to grab your stuff and go. Let's have coffee and you can tell me what's happening."

She wanted to decline the invitation, until she looked into his blue eyes and started tingling all over. Then she followed him inside.

"Nothing's happening, really," she said. "I've been busy with yards and pools, landscaping." She shrugged.

She wasn't sure how much he heard because his gaze was glued to her mouth. "I've missed you like hell," he said.

"I missed you, Gabe," she whispered, fighting the urge to throw her arms around him. He looked incredible with locks of his black hair falling on his forehead, a shadow of stubble on his jaw. The sight of him made her heart race.

"We wouldn't have any kind of future together, would we?"

His question hurt because it just emphasized their differences. She shook her head. "No, because I still can't take your lifestyle," she said, thinking about her brother's needless death, "and I know you can't give it up." They stared at each other in silence for a moment and she felt her heart break once again because there was no hope for a future together.

"Ah, Meg, come here," he said.

Her heart thudded while she walked into his arms eagerly and raised her face for his kiss. It felt like coming home.

It took a few moments before she realized her phone was buzzing in her pocket.

"Gabe, wait," she said. "My phone." She pulled it out and frowned. "It's my dad, and he doesn't call when I'm at work, which is where he thinks I am. I better take it."

She walked away and talked softly and in minutes returned. "Gabe, I have to go right now. Last week my grandfather fell and he broke his arm and two ribs. The doctors in Colorado said he could travel. My parents want to bring him back here where all his doctors are. Dad and Mom are leaving to go get him as soon as they can get ready. I told them I'd go with them. Mom doesn't like highway driving and it's stormy all through western Kansas and into Colorado."

"Meg, let me fly all of you there. My plane is

big enough to get him and bring him back here. Where in Colorado?"

"It's Colorado Springs. But we can't go in your plane."

"Yes, you can. It'll be easier on him and save at least a day of driving. All of you can go. My plane isn't little until you compare it with a Boeing 747."

"I can't do that, Gabe. I can't fly." Already she could feel her heart pounding, just at the thought.

He must have seen the fear in her eyes because he nodded. "You don't have to go. Your folks can come with me. Let me call the airport and get some information and get things ready."

She frowned, staring at him. She didn't want to fly and she didn't want to risk her family, either. On the other hand, Gabe was right. It would be easier on all of them.

In a few minutes, Gabe returned. "The weather is stormy, but it's okay to fly. The plane will be ready shortly. I'm flying and I have a copilot who works for me. He'll meet me at the airport. Call your folks and tell them I have a limo to take us to the airport. They won't object to flying with me, will they? If they do, let me talk to your dad."

"I'll call and you can talk to Dad." In minutes she handed the phone to Gabe and walked away as he began to tell her father about his pilot qualifications. She stood by a window. It was sunny and a clear day without wind in Dallas. How far could they go before they hit stormy weather? She wound her fingers together and dreaded the flight, but made her decision. She wanted to go along.

Gabe turned to her and held out her phone. "Your folks are going. As soon as the limo gets here, I'll leave and pick them up." Gabe walked to her and placed his hands on her shoulders. "You don't have to go, Meg, but there's something you need to know. You're too vibrant to go through life being afraid. Life is full of risks, but some are bigger than others. You have to take some risks. You do when you go to work. You do when you fall in love." He dropped his hands and turned away. "I've got to get ready."

"Wait," she called out. "I'm coming."

She saw the smile he tried to hide before he went to pack his things.

A few minutes later she saw a black limo coming up his drive. They went outside and as soon as it stopped, the driver stepped out.

"Thanks, Gene, for getting here so quickly. Meg, this is our driver, Gene Gray. Gene, this is Miss Aldridge. She can give you her parents' address."

By the time they'd picked up her parents and made it to the airport, her heart was pounding so hard she thought it'd burst. But she felt remotely better when she saw the size of the plane.

"Gabe, this plane is a lot bigger than what Hank flew."

"I have two planes. This one is the bigger one. I have one like Hank's that I fly to the ranch."

She felt slightly better that she wasn't flying in a tin can. As Gabe took charge, she followed his directions and in no time she and her parents were on board, seated and comfortable in a plush lounge.

Gabe turned to her. "Okay?"

"So far." She even managed a small smile. "I have to tell you, you've impressed my dad."

"Good," he said. "Once we're up, the flight attendant will pass out drinks, pillows and magazines," he told her. "Just relax."

Meg buckled up as Gabe made his way to the cockpit. Minutes later she gripped the seat with white knuckles as the plane picked up speed going down the runway. She held her breath until they were finally airborne, lifting quickly, making a wide circle and heading north.

They had good weather until they were over Kansas. Gabe kept them posted at regular intervals and they were making good time when they flew into clouds. Cold fear gripped her and she couldn't relax. Her parents had fallen asleep and Meg wished she was able to do the same.

The flight became bumpy and she hated every jolt. She couldn't see out the window because of the thick gray clouds surrounding them and she couldn't imagine how Gabe could tell where he was flying, even with instruments and electronics and everything else he had. And how would they land?

Her mother woke up and looked at her, wide-eyed as she glanced outside. She looked at Meg's dad and then leaned toward Meg. "Are you all right?"

"I'm fine," Meg lied. She hated the flight and wanted it to be over and dreaded having to go back. They weren't flying back until the next day and she prayed the weather would be better then.

For the next hour, the plane hit more turbulence and she clutched the seat and closed her eyes. By the time the flight became smooth again, they were landing.

Gabe stood waiting as she stepped to the door behind her parents. He moved close to slip his arm around her waist. "How're you doing? You made it."

"Barely."

"But you did it. It might get easier." He smiled at her and squeezed her lightly.

He had a limo waiting for them that took them straight to Meg's aunt's house, where Gabe met her aunt and uncle and saw her grandmother again and spoke to her grandfather briefly. He was seated in a comfortable chair with his arm in a sling, the only obvious sign of his fall.

When Gabe got up to leave, Meg followed him outside and closed the door behind her. The air was cool even though it was summer, and she wrapped her arms around her middle. "Thank you for flying us here, Gabe."

"I was glad to. Tomorrow the weather should be good and the flight will be better."

She didn't want to say goodbye to him, but she knew he couldn't stay. "Well, I better go back in." She turned to open the door but he stopped her.

He pulled her to him, flush against him, and his body seemed to burn right through her. "Damn, it's good to be with you, even if it was just for that plane ride. I've missed you."

Her heart thudded and she held him tightly. "I've missed you, Gabe," she answered solemnly. She didn't want to miss him, didn't want to be so glad to have his arms around her. But she couldn't deny that was how she felt.

He leaned away to look at her and then he

kissed her, and she kissed him in return, unable to resist him.

"I'll see you in the morning." She watched him get into the limo and it drove away before she went back in to join the family.

The next day the flight home was uneventful. The clouds were white puffs in a blue sky, the flight was smooth and her parents and grandparents were happily talking. She sat back in the plush, comfortable lounge and tried to relax.

Was she throwing away a lifetime of happiness because she was too scared to live and take some risks? She thought about Gabe at the controls. He hadn't been a wreck worrying about the weather yesterday. He was right about life being filled with risks. Would her fears cause her to miss out on a life with the man she loved?

Maybe she was focusing too much on dangers and not looking at what she would miss.

She loved Gabe with all her heart. Would his love be worth taking risks? Could she live with his wild ways if it meant also living with his love? He wasn't into commitment—could she accept that?

She couldn't answer her own questions, but she began to do a lot of thinking.

All her worries about this flight had been for nothing and it was far better than driving through blinding rain for days. Was she going through life with an unfounded anxiety about ordinary living? Not to mention some things that weren't so ordinary—like Gabe's rodeo bulls. She wondered if she was cutting herself out of what she really loved by being afraid to take some risks, and if she could find a way to live with Gabe's fearless ways.

After her parents and grandparents were home, she rode to Gabe's house in the limo. Her car was still at his house and she had to get her bag, as well.

As soon as they stepped inside his house and Gabe closed the door, he took her into his arms. "Ah, Meg, come here," he said.

Her heart thudded as she went into his arms eagerly and raised her face for his kiss, knowing exactly where this would lead.

* * *

Over two hours later, she shifted in bed as she lay in the crook of his arm.

He caressed her shoulder lightly. "Darlin', I've had time to think about us. I don't like life without you."

His words thrilled her and scared her.

"Gabe, I thought about us on the way back today and maybe you're right. Maybe my anxieties are cutting me out of what I want most. But that would be a huge change for me and I can't just flip a switch." She pulled back so she could see his face. "I can't suddenly say I don't care if you ride bulls or your Harley or fly your planes, but I do feel differently about it. Give me some time and let's both think about being together."

A smile broke out across his face. "Darlin', that's progress. Take all the time you need." His expression grew more somber. "But I hope it's not a lot of time. I really miss you."

"We need some space to think about what we mean to each other, Gabe."

"So does this mean moving in with me is out of the question?" he teased.

"Moving in with you would be a giant step for me. Besides, you aren't into a lasting commitment. If I lived with you, I'd fall in love more and more every day. And then someday it would be over for you, and then what happens to me? I've got to think about dealing with that."

It didn't go unnoticed by her that he remained quiet. He merely held her closer, against the beating of his heart.

"Right now, Gabe, I need to get home. I had appointments I missed at work." She kissed him again and rolled away to step out of bed, go shower and dress.

Later, when she stood at his door after they kissed goodbye, she smiled at him. "Gabe, once again, you were the knight to my rescue. Thank you."

"You think about us and you call me, darlin'. But just remember that I really want you and I'm going to miss you more than I can tell you."

"And you do the same, Gabe."

She knew she should learn to live with and accept more risks in her life because some of her worries existed more in her imagination. But not all of them. There was no getting away from some of the risks he took. But there was another issue keeping them apart. Could she live with him, love him more than ever and then have him walk away sometime in the future?

If she moved in with him, she wanted it to be permanent and she knew he didn't. And if it wasn't permanent she worried that would eventually hurt her way more than telling him goodbye now. Did she want to risk a giant hurt for a month or two of living with him and then having him leave her? He always left the women in his life. Would she be fooling herself if she thought she would be different?

Eleven

Gabe spent the next week on his ranch doing the hardest physical work he could find. He had a call from his office in Dallas about a large business complex in Houston his company had for sale and complications because the buyers wanted possession within the next two months. He handed the call off to someone at the office. He had no desire to sit on the phone for hours.

At night he hated going home. The house was empty and his bed was empty. He missed Meg more each day instead of less. He caught himself at times during the day looking at her pictures that were on his phone. "I love you and I miss you," he said to the pictures.

As he worked putting up a new gate, he stopped, wiped his forehead and stared into space. Meg had said she would rethink her worries about his lifestyle and he had told her to call him, but so far he hadn't heard anything. His lifestyle was still between them and keeping Meg from moving in. Could he change anything, give up anything that might make her compromise? He picked up a board to saw it in two while he thought about the things he wanted to do the most, the things he enjoyed the most, the things she might consider the most dangerous.

And what about his lack of commitment? She worried about moving in and falling in love with no promise of permanence. She knew his reputation for never being serious. He'd dated scores of women, but he had never really been in love—until now. Yes, he could finally admit it. He loved Meg.

She had been part of his life forever but now it was different. He wanted more than a friend, and he wanted her more than ever. He was in love and there was no going back to the life he'd had before she showed up at his door. But something had to give. What could he concede? And would she meet him halfway?

He wanted her in his arms, in his bed, and he hadn't slept well since he'd told her goodbye. She'd said she'd missed him, but she had a way of bouncing back in life and going blithely on with what she was involved in and never letting anything really get her down. He thought he could do that, too, until he fell in love with her. For all he knew, she could be dating someone else. That thought sent a cold chill running down his spine.

"Damn, Meg," he said, tossing his tools in the back of his pickup and sliding behind the wheel. He intended to put an end to this right now.

Meg sat at her desk at home a little after ten o'clock at night. She stared at landscape plans for a large yard in an exclusive, gated residential area. She couldn't concentrate on her work. Her mind continually went back to Gabe. She stood up and walked to the kitchen to get another glass of water, lost in memories and thoughts of him.

She missed him. She couldn't concentrate. She didn't want to go out and she avoided going to visit her parents because she didn't want to answer questions and her mother worried because she thought Meg was losing weight.

She picked up the old brown bear on the kitchen counter. "I miss him," she whispered to the bear, its glass eyes staring back at her.

She got a text message, saw it was from Gabe and read swiftly:

I'm on your porch. I need to see you.

Shocked, she dropped the bear and ran toward the front door to yank it open. She couldn't believe it. Gabe stood in front of her and she threw herself into his arms, turning her face up to kiss him as he embraced her.

His arms were tight around her and while he kissed her hard he walked her backward inside where he kicked the door closed. Her heart thudded and joy and sorrow warred within her.

He held her away to look at her. "I've missed you too much. We have to do something. I've thought about what I can give up, to see what you can live with."

Startled, she stared at him as her heart started pounding and joy came rushing back. "You really did that? You'd do that for me?"

"Yes, I will because I don't want to live without you. I need you in my life. You're necessary now, darlin'. I'm hoping for a sort of compromise here."

"Good. 'Cause I've been doing some thinking of my own. I'm up for a compromise, too. What can you give up?"

"Motorcycles. I've sold mine."

"Oh, my goodness," she said, shocked, and a thrill tickled her to her toes. "Seriously?"

"I'm serious, darlin'. I've never been more serious. Life is hell without you. I love you."

She smiled a huge smile. "You love me? The great love-is-not-for-me Gabe Callahan loves me?" She loved him, and she loved teasing him.

"Yes, darlin', I do." He swept her up in his arms again and gave her a kiss that proved it. Then he set her down and grinned down at her.

"Gabe, I love you with all my heart and I've been miserable without you."

He took her hands in his. "Then let's get through the official stuff so we can get to the good part." She laughed. "So what can you live with?"

"Well, I've been trying to think what I can live with. Believe it or not, your planes will head the list."

"That's good. I get to keep my planes. We're a step closer to getting together." He took off his hat and flicked it onto her sofa. "And I'll give up bull riding in rodeos."

"Oh, Gabe, really? That's enough. Well, maybe one more thing. Don't drive way, way over the speed limit."

"I can live with that. I promise."

Suddenly, she threw her arms around him. "You'd do all that for me? I love you so."

Laughing, he caught her and held her tightly as he leaned close to kiss her. Moments later she pushed away slightly to gaze up at him. "Gabe, I don't want to live in fear. You've shown me that. But there's still one more thing. I can't get so tied to you that I'd never want you to leave, not while you don't want a part of anything permanent."

"Don't decide what I want and what I don't want. Leave that to me." In one smooth motion he picked her off her feet and carried her to the bedroom. He set her on her feet again and looked down at her.

"There's no violin playing, no roses and no fancy setting, but this time I mean it." He went down on one knee in front of her and she thought her heart would burst from her chest when she saw the sincerity in his eyes. "Meg, will you marry me?"

With a screech of joy, she flung her arms around him and kissed him. She didn't need a violin to make this the most perfect proposal she could ever hear. All she needed was Gabe telling her this time it was for real.

He pulled back and gazed into her eyes. "I take it that's a yes?"

She threw her head back and spun around. "Oh, yes!" She vaulted into his arms.

"Wait a minute, Meg. I just realized I'm not doing this right. I should have called your dad and told him I want to marry you, but I was afraid it would cause real problems for us, and also that you might turn me down."

"It's not going to cause problems and I'm not turning you down. Maybe this will end the silly feud," she said, laughing and trying to stand on tiptoe to kiss him while she unbuttoned his shirt.

"Wait a minute, my hot lover." He reached into his pocket and brought out a box tied with a ribbon. "Darlin', I want to spend a lifetime telling you and showing you how much I love you. This is a token of that love."

Her hands were trembling when she took the box from him. She could hardly think straight, she was so dazzled that she would be spending the rest of her life with the man she loved and had always loved. She steadied herself enough to untie the ribbon and open the box. She gasped as she looked at a dazzling diamond solitaire on a band covered in smaller diamonds. "Gabe, this is beautiful. And it's a rock."

"Ten carats. I want the world to know you're my lady and I love you with all my heart. And darlin', I promise to be a better dad than the one I had."

He took the ring and held her hand, looking down at her. "Meg, I can't ever really show you how much I love you, but I want to spend a lifetime trying. You're my best friend, my world. I love you."

"I love you, Gabe. You're my best friend and always have been, and now you're my love," she said, gazing into his blue eyes.

He slipped the ring on her finger and then drew her to him to kiss her. She held him tightly, certain this cowboy had her heart completely and they had a future together that would be filled with joy, laughter and love.

* * * * *

MILLS & BOON®
Large Print – June 2017

ROMANCE

The Last Di Sione Claims His Prize	Maisey Yates
Bought to Wear the Billionaire's Ring	Cathy Williams
The Desert King's Blackmailed Bride	Lynne Graham
Bride by Royal Decree	Caitlin Crews
The Consequence of His Vengeance	Jennie Lucas
The Sheikh's Secret Son	Maggie Cox
Acquired by Her Greek Boss	Chantelle Shaw
The Sheikh's Convenient Princess	Liz Fielding
The Unforgettable Spanish Tycoon	Christy McKellen
The Billionaire of Coral Bay	Nikki Logan
Her First-Date Honeymoon	Katrina Cudmore

HISTORICAL

The Harlot and the Sheikh	Marguerite Kaye
The Duke's Secret Heir	Sarah Mallory
Miss Bradshaw's Bought Betrothal	Virginia Heath
Sold to the Viking Warrior	Michelle Styles
A Marriage of Rogues	Margaret Moore

MEDICAL

White Christmas for the Single Mum	Susanne Hampton
A Royal Baby for Christmas	Scarlet Wilson
Playboy on Her Christmas List	Carol Marinelli
The Army Doc's Baby Bombshell	Sue MacKay
The Doctor's Sleigh Bell Proposal	Susan Carlisle
Christmas with the Single Dad	Louisa Heaton

0517 GEN STD LP

MILLS & BOON®
Hardback – July 2017

ROMANCE

The Pregnant Kavakos Bride	Sharon Kendrick
The Billionaire's Secret Princess	Caitlin Crews
Sicilian's Baby of Shame	Carol Marinelli
The Secret Kept from the Greek	Susan Stephens
A Ring to Secure His Crown	Kim Lawrence
Wedding Night with Her Enemy	Melanie Milburne
Salazar's One-Night Heir	Jennifer Hayward
Claiming His Convenient Fiancée	Natalie Anderson
The Mysterious Italian Houseguest	Scarlet Wilson
Bound to Her Greek Billionaire	Rebecca Winters
Their Baby Surprise	Katrina Cudmore
The Marriage of Inconvenience	Nina Singh
The Surrogate's Unexpected Miracle	Alison Roberts
Convenient Marriage, Surprise Twins	Amy Ruttan
The Doctor's Secret Son	Janice Lynn
Reforming the Playboy	Karin Baine
Their Double Baby Gift	Louisa Heaton
Saving Baby Amy	Annie Claydon
The Baby Favour	Andrea Laurence
Lone Star Baby Scandal	Lauren Canan

MILLS & BOON®
Large Print – July 2017

ROMANCE

Secrets of a Billionaire's Mistress	Sharon Kendrick
Claimed for the De Carrillo Twins	Abby Green
The Innocent's Secret Baby	Carol Marinelli
The Temporary Mrs Marchetti	Melanie Milburne
A Debt Paid in the Marriage Bed	Jennifer Hayward
The Sicilian's Defiant Virgin	Susan Stephens
Pursued by the Desert Prince	Dani Collins
Return of Her Italian Duke	Rebecca Winters
The Millionaire's Royal Rescue	Jennifer Faye
Proposal for the Wedding Planner	Sophie Pembroke
A Bride for the Brooding Boss	Bella Bucannon

HISTORICAL

Surrender to the Marquess	Louise Allen
Heiress on the Run	Laura Martin
Convenient Proposal to the Lady	Julia Justiss
Waltzing with the Earl	Catherine Tinley
At the Warrior's Mercy	Denise Lynn

MEDICAL

Falling for Her Wounded Hero	Marion Lennox
The Surgeon's Baby Surprise	Charlotte Hawkes
Santiago's Convenient Fiancée	Annie O'Neil
Alejandro's Sexy Secret	Amy Ruttan
The Doctor's Diamond Proposal	Annie Claydon
Weekend with the Best Man	Leah Martyn

0617 GEN STD LP